The Yellow Umbrella

Ruskin Bond is known for his signature simplistic and witty writing style. He is the author of several bestselling short stories, novellas, collections, essays and children's books; and has contributed a number of poems and articles to various magazines and anthologies. At the age of twenty-three, he won the prestigious John Llewellyn Rhys Prize for his first novel, *The Room on the Roof*. He was also the recipient of the Padma Shri in 1999, Lifetime Achievement Award by the Delhi Government in 2012 and the Padma Bhushan in 2014.

Born in 1934, Ruskin Bond grew up in Jamnagar, Shimla, New Delhi and Dehradun. Apart from three years in the UK, he has spent all his life in India, and now lives in Landour, Mussoorie, with his adopted family.

RUSKIN BOND

The Yellow Umbrella

RUPA

Published by
Rupa Publications India Pvt. Ltd 2022
7/16, Ansari Road, Daryaganj
New Delhi 110002

Sales centres:
Allahabad Bengaluru Chennai
Hyderabad Jaipur Kathmandu
Kolkata Mumbai

ISBN: 978-93-5520-634-3

First impression 2022

10 9 8 7 6 5 4 3 2 1

Moral right of the author has been asserted.

Printed in India

CONTENTS

INTRODUCTION

Reminiscing is often how we keep our personal histories alive. By collecting tokens of a time long past—letters sent to us by friends, parents and ex-lovers, a single pressed flower in a teenager's diary, a card sent by a grandparent, movie ticket stubs—we create our own museums of history. These remind us of who we used to be, and can often serve as reminders of who we wanted to be.

It is not just things stored in a box that help us remember but also the people we have met along the way. Often, to make a decision that'll help us stay true to ourselves, we call a friend that has known us all our lives. So many people, places and things make up the history—one that lives all around us and in us. The fragrance of a home-cooked meal can remind you of your grandmother, a song on the radio can remind you of your first heartbreak—it's the easiest thing, reminiscing.

This book is a compilation of such recollections, some fictionalized, others, verbatim. A dilapidated hotel in a forgotten town; a lost-but-not-forgotten love affair; some snippets of childhood adventures, and friends we make along the way. It has, in its motley of souvenirs, a new story about a postman, who brought a young writer his all-important cheques and letters, and had a presence as bright as his yellow umbrella.

Ruskin Bond

THE YELLOW UMBRELLA

The postman knocks—or used to, in the old days when I lived in Maplewood Lodge, down in the forest on the outskirts of Mussoorie. Now the courier services have taken over, and the postman is something of a rarity, but back in the '60s and 70s, I would always be looking out for him, because he brought me cheques from publishers and magazines, and in those days it was the only mode of payment apart from the occasional money order. I was making a living entirely from my writing, and those 'cheques in the mail' were essential for my survival.

Prakash was my postman for two or three years his daily beat brought him from the post office on the Mall to the school on the ridge above my cottage, a walk of about two and a half miles. He was nearing sixty, on the verge of retirement, and the long walk would tire him out.

I had been in the cottage just three or four days when he came trudging down the forest path with a couple of letters for me. I was at my desk on the verandah when I heard a stentorian voice calling: 'Postman, postman!' I got up from my desk. He looked at my typewriter.

'This is your work, your office?' he asked.

'Yes, I'am a writer,' I said.

'No you are a typer,' he said.

'You mean a typist? I do my writing on this typewriter. (In those days I used to type my stories.)

'So you are a typer-writer,' he insisted.

And from that day on he always addressed he as Mr Typer-writer.

Well, I didn't mind as long as I got my letters. And he was very regular, turning up every day (except holidays) around noon, calling out. 'Postman! Letters for Mr Typer-writer!' He had some difficulty pronouncing my real name.

He would usually find me at my desk or in the ting garden where I was trying to grow snapdragons and petunias. On hot days he would ask me for a glass of water, and after he had quenched his thirst he would sit on the low garden wall for five or ten minutes and bring me up to date on what was happening in the town. A movie was being made on the Mall, and there was much excitement because the beautiful Hema Malini was in town. Or something more mundane such as a leopard having been seen on the Camel's Back Road, or a beauty contest underway at the Savoy. I seldom went into town, so Prakash the postman was my local newspaper.

The months passed quietly, the seasons changed, my work progressed. Those all-important cheques arrived from time to time, so did the winter rains and a fall of snow. Prakash had a rough voice but he wasn't very strong, and in his old, frayed overcoat he was beginning to look older than his years. Instant of a glass of water, I gave him a glass of hot sweet tea, and he would perk up and plod back up the hill to his quarters in the town. He was married but his wife lived in their village on the next range. She had to look after his old mother and a cow and a couple of goats.

'I will retire soon,' he told me, 'and then I will get another cow and maybe a mule to bring our milk and vegetables to Mussoorie. Big business!'

When summer come again he abandoned his overcoat are

started wearing a cap to shield him from the sun. Then, when the monsoon arrived, he started carrying an umbrella. It was shabby and torn and did not give him much protection. And the rains were heavy that year.

'Won't the post office give you a decent umbrella?' I asked.

'They gave me this one five years ago,' he said, 'Now they don't have a budget for umbrellas.'

'Well, I'll get you one,' I said 'I'm going into town tomorrow, and I'll get you a good umbrella.'

'That's very kind of you,' said Prakash.' I would like a blue umbrella.'

'Why blue?'

He told me that he had often seen a little village girl, Binya coming from or going to school, and she had a pretty blue umbrella. He wanted one just like it!

'Well, I'll see what I can find,' I said. And I walked into town, looking for a blue umbrella.

But the umbrella shops had all run out of blue umbrellas. Suddenly they had become very popular.

I didn't think Prakash would care for an ordinary black umbrella, So I settled for a bright yellow umbrella, and the following day, when he arrived with his old umbrella blown inside out by a strong wind, I presented him with the yellow umbrella.

'Yellow is the colour of the sun,' I said. It will keep you sunny and cheerful!'

He accepted it graciously and carried it about wherever he went, even when the rains were over. You could tell when he was coming because of that blob of bright yellow moving about on the hillside.

Then one day, in the middle of October, someone else arrived with my post.

He was a young man, healthy dressed, very polite. 'Your

letters, sir, I'm the now postman.'

It was quite a shock.

'What happened to Prakash?' I asked anxiously, 'I hope he isn't sick.'

'He's fine, sir. He took his retirement pension and went back to his village.'

'Oh, I see.' I was a little disappointed that he hadn't told me he was going, but he was probably in a hurry to buy that cow. The new postman was fine, and I did not expect to see Prakash again.

It was late October. I'd been working hard, and I felt like getting away from typewriter, even if it was only for a couple of days. I was a good walker and had done some trekking over the years. I decided to take a long walk to Dhanaulti, where there was an old forest rest house set amidst deodars and horse-chestnuts.

In those days there was no motor road to Dhanaulti, just a footpath used by pilgrims on their arduous trek to Gangotri. Dhanaulti was about twenty miles from my cottage, and I expected to be there by evening if I walked at a steady pace. My friend and helper, Pran Singh, made some sandwiches for me and filled a water-bottle with lemon juice; these went into my haversack (the modern backpack had yet to be invented) and I set off cheerfully, hoping to enjoy the sparkling autumn air and the wonderful views from the winding path to Dhanolti.

I'd covered about five miles, past the village of Suakholi, when I found the path blocked by a herd of goats, and order to avoid them I left the narrow path and scrambled up the slope of the hill, made slippery by fallen pine needles. On my way down I slipped and fell, twisting my ankle, I wasn't badly hurt, but the ankle was painful, and I continued limping along, wishing I'd brought along a stout walking-stick.

Still, I struggled on, as I was now about half way to Dhanaulti, and when I saw some wayside huts about half a mile distant, I decided I'd rest in the village and then decide whether to go or not.

As I approached, I noticed a large yellow blob outside one of the shacks. It was a yellow umbrella! And beneath it, sheltering from the sun was Prakash, my old postman.

As soon as he saw me, he got up, exclaiming: 'Typer-writer sir! What are you doing here?'

'Just taking a walk. Is this your village?'

'Yes, my fields are just below. But you have hurt yourself, come and sit down. Better still, come inside and rest.'

His small tile-roofed dwelling was first off the road. It was two-storied, the ground floor being reserved for his cows. Yes, there were now two of them.

He took me upstairs and made me comfortable on an old cane chair, then called for his wife and asked her to make us some tea. She was a round, plump, jolly woman who was delighted to have an unexpected visitor. The tea was followed by hot pakoras and walnuts from their own walnut tree.

'You have sprained your ankle,' said Prakash. 'See, it is quite swollen. You should not walk any further. Better to stay the night.'

But I know that Prakash would not have a spare cot or even a spare mattress, so I said 'I'll manage, it's not too bad.'

Just then a pack of mules arrived, on its way to Mussoorie, the mules loaded with sacks of beans and radishes. The mule-driver was singing the latest Hindi hit song.

'Hey, Melaram!' shouted Prakash. 'Do you have space on one of your mules?'

'For a friend of yours there will be space,' answered the mule-drives.

'Then deliver my friend the Typer-writer to the first doctor you find in Mussoorie.'

'At your command,' said Melaram. 'It shall be done.' He brought over one of his mules, transferred its load to another mule, and made a saddle of sorts out of empty gunny-bags. There were straggled on to the patient animal, and I was helped on to it by the two men, while Prakash's wife looked on with unconcealed amusement.

It was the first time I had taken a ride on a mule, and I hoped there would not be another. Two hours of riding a mule can give you a very sore bottom.

'Come again, Typer-writer sir,' said Prakash, and we set off at a marry trot, the mule-driver in the lead, followed by my mount and several others. I looked back to see Prakash waving to me, holding up the yellow umbrella, which had turned to burnished gold in the setting sun.

There's an old saying, 'One good turn deserves another'. A bit of a cliché but true. There's such a thing as a law of compensation, a sort of Karma, that works best in this life. Kindness begets kindness, and never mind the sore bottom.

ADVENTURES IN READING

1
BEAUTY IN SMALL BOOKS

You don't see them so often now, those tiny books and almanacs—genuine pocketbooks—once so popular with our parents and grandparents; much smaller than the average paperback, often smaller than the palm of the hand. With the advent of coffee-table books, new books keep growing bigger and bigger, rivalling tombstones! And one day, like Alice after drinking from the wrong bottle, they will reach the ceiling and won't have anywhere else to go. The average publisher, who apparently believes that large profits are linked to large books, must look upon these old miniatures with amusement or scorn. They were not meant for a coffee table, true. They were meant for true book-lovers and readers, for they took up very little space—you could slip them into your pocket without any discomfort, either to you or to the pocket.

I have a small collection of these little books, treasured over the years. Foremost is my father's prayer-book and psalter, with his name, 'Aubrey Bond, Lovedale, 1917', inscribed on the inside back cover. Lovedale is a school in the Nilgiri Hills in south India, where, as a young man, he did his teacher's training. He gave it to me soon after I went to a boarding school in Shimla, in 1944, and my own name is inscribed on it in his beautiful handwriting.

Another beautiful little prayer-book in my collection is called *The Finger Prayer Book*. Bound in soft leather, it is about the same length and breadth as the average middle finger. Replete with psalms, it is the complete book of common prayer and not an abridgement; a marvel of miniature book production.

Not much larger is a delicate item in calf-leather, *The Humour of Charles Lamb*. It fits into my wallet and often stays there. It has a tiny portrait of the great essayist, followed by some thirty to forty extracts from his essays, such as this favourite of mine: 'Every dead man must take upon himself to be lecturing me with his odious truism, that "Such as he is now, I must shortly be". Not so shortly friend, perhaps as thou imaginest. In the meantime, I am alive. I move about. I am worth twenty of thee. Know thy betters!'

No fatalist, Lamb. He made no compromise with Father Time. He affirmed that in age we must be as glowing and tempestuous as in youth! And yet Lamb is thought to be an old-fashioned writer.

Another favourite among my 'little' books is *The Pocket Trivet, An Anthology for Optimists*, published by *The Morning Post* newspaper in 1932. But what is a trivet? The unenlightened may well ask. Well, it's a stand for a small pot or kettle, fixed securely over a grate. To be right as a trivet is to be perfectly right. Just right, like the short sayings in this book, which is further enlivened by a number of charming woodcuts based on the seventeenth-century originals; such as the illustration of a moth hovering over a candle flame and below it the legend—'I seeke mine own hurt.'

But the sayings are mostly of a cheering nature, such as Emerson's 'Hitch your wagon to a star!' or the West Indian proverb: 'Every day no Christmas, an' every day no rainy day.'

My book of trivets is a happy example of much concentrated wisdom being collected in a small space—the beauty separated from the dross. It helps me to forget the dilapidated building in which I live and to look instead, at the ever-changing cloud patterns as seen from my bedroom windows. There is no end to the shapes made by the clouds, or to the stories they set off in my head. We don't have to circle the world in order to find beauty and fulfilment. After all, most of living has to happen in the mind. And, to quote one anonymous sage from my trivet, 'The world is only the size of each man's head.'

2
WRITTEN BY HAND

Amongst the current fraternity of writers, I must be that very rare person—an author who actually writes by hand!

Soon after the invention of the typewriter, most editors and publishers understandably refused to look at any mansucript that was handwritten. A decade or two earlier, when Dickens and Balzac had submitted their hefty manuscrips in longhand, no one had raised any objection. Had their handwriting been awful, their manuscripts would still have been read. Fortunately for all concerned, most writers, famous or obscure, took pains over their handwriting. For some, it was an art in itself, and many of those early manuscripts are a pleasure to look at and read.

And it wasn't only authors who wrote with an elegant hand. Parents and grandparents of most of us had distinctive styles of their own. I still have my father's last letter, written to me when I was at boarding school in Shimla some fifty years ago. He used large, beautifully formed letters, and his thoughts seemed to have the same flow and clarity as his handwriting.

In his letter he advises me (then a nine-year-old) about my

own handwriting: 'I wanted to write before about your writing. Ruskin...sometimes I get letters from you in very small writing, as if you wanted to squeeze everything into one sheet of letter paper. It is not good for you or for your eyes, to get into the habit of writing too small... Try and form a larger style of handwriting—use more paper if necessary!'

I did my best to follow his advice, and I'm glad to report that after nearly forty years of the writing life, most people can still read my handwriting!

Word-processors are all the rage now, and I have no objection to these mechanical aids any more than I have to my old Olympia typewriter, made in 1956 and still going strong. Although I do all my writing in longhand, I follow the conventions by typing a second draft. But I would not enjoy my writing if I had to do it straight on to a machine. It isn't just the pleasure of writing longhand. I like taking my notebooks and writing-pads to odd places. This particular essay is being written on the steps of my small cottage facing Pari Tibba (Fairy Hill). Part of the reason for sitting here is that there is a new postman on this route, and I don't want him to miss me.

For a freelance writer, the postman is almost as important as a publisher. I could, of course, sit here doing nothing, but as I have pencil and paper with me, and feel like using them, I shall write until the postman comes and maybe after he has gone, too! There is really no way in which I could set up a word-processor on these steps.

There are a number of favourite places where I do my writing. One is under the chestnut tree on the slope above the cottage. Word-processors were not designed keeping mountain slopes in mind. But armed with a pen (or pencil) and paper, I can lie on the grass and write for hours. On one occasion, last month, I did take my typewriter into the garden, and I am still trying to extricate an acorn from under the keys, while the roller seems permanently stained yellow with some fine pollen-dust from the deodar trees.

My friends keep telling me about all the wonderful things I can do with a word-processor, but they haven't got around to finding me one that I can take to bed, for that is another place where I do much of my writing—especially on cold winter nights, when it is impossible to keep the cottage warm.

While the wind howls outside, and snow piles up on the window-sill, I am warm under my quilt, writing pad on my knees, ballpoint pen at the ready. And if, next day, the weather is warm and sunny, these simple aids will accompany me on a long walk, ready for instant use should I wish to record an incident, a prospect, a conversation or simply a train of thought.

When I think of the great eighteenth- and nineteenth-century writers, scratching away with their quill pens, filling hundreds of pages every month, I am amazed to find that their handwriting did not deteriorate into the sort of hieroglyphics that often make up the average doctor's prescription today. They knew they had to write legibly, if only for the sake of the typesetters.

Both Dickens and Thackeray had good, clear, flourishing styles. (Thackeray was a clever illustrator, too.) Somerset Maugham had an upright, legible hand. Churchill's neat handwriting never wavered, even when he was under stress. I like the bold, clear, straighforward hand of Abraham Lincoln; it mirrors the man. Mahatma Gandhi, another great soul who fell to the assassin's bullet, had many similarities of both handwriting and outlook.

Not everyone had a beautiful hand. King Henry VIII had an untidy scrawl, but then, he was not a man of much refinement. Guy Fawkes, who tried to blow up the British Parliament, had a very shaky hand. With such a quiver, no wonder he failed in his attempt! Hitler's signature is ugly, as you would expect. And Napoleon's doesn't seem to know where to stop; how much like the man!

I think my father was right when he said handwriting was often the key to a man's character, and that large well-formed letters went with an uncluttered mind. Florence Nightingale had a lovely handwriting, the hand of a caring person. And there were many like her, amongst our forebears.

3
WORDS AND PICTURES

When I was a small boy, no Christmas was really complete unless my Christmas stocking contained several recent issues of my favourite comic paper. If today my friends complain that I am too voracious a reader of books, they have only these comics to blame; for they were the origin, if not of my tastes in reading, then certainly of the reading habit itself.

I like to think that my conversion to comics began at the age of five, with a comic strip on the children's page of *The Statesman*. In the late 1930s, Benji, whose head later appeared only on the Benji League badge, had a strip to himself; I don't remember his adventures very clearly, but every day (or was it once a week?) I would cut out the Benji strip and paste it into a scrapbook. Two years later, this scrapbook, bursting with the adventures of Benji, accompanied me to boarding school, where, of course, it passed through several hands before finally passing into limbo.

Of course comics did not form the only reading matter that found its way into my Christmas stocking. Before 1 was eight, I had read Peter Pan, Alice and most of Mr Midshipman Easy; but I had also consumed thousands of comic-papers which were, after all, slim affairs and mostly pictorial, 'certain little penny books radiant with gold and rich with bad pictures', as Leigh Hunt described the children's papers of his own time.

But though they were mostly pictorial, comics in those days did have a fair amount of reading matter, too. *The Hosspur, Wizard, Magnet* (a victim of the Second World War) and *Champion* contained stories woven round certain popular characters. In Champion, which I read regularly right through my prep school years, there was Rockfist Rogan, Royal Air Force (R.A.F.), a pugilist who managed to combine boxing with bombing, and Fireworks Flynn, a footballer who always scored the winning goal in the last two minutes of play

Billy Bunter has, of course, become one of the immortals— almost a subject for literary and social historians. Quite recently, *The Times Literary Supplement* devoted its first two pages to an analysis of the Bunter stories. Eminent lawyers and doctors still look back nostalgically to the arrival of the weekly *Magnet*; they are now the principal customers for the special souvenir edition of the first issue of the *Magnet*, recently reprinted in facsimile. Bunter, 'forever young', has become a folk-hero. He is seen on stage, screen and television, and is even quoted in the House of Commons.

From this, I take courage. My only regret is that I did not preserve my own early comics—not because of any bibliophilic value which they might possess today, but because of my sentimental regard for early influences in art and literature.

The first venture in children's publishing, in 1774 was a comic of sorts. In that year, John Newberry brought out:

> According to Act of Parliament (neatly bound and gilt): A Little Pretty Pocket-Book, intended for the Instruction and Amusement of Little Master Tommy and Pretty Miss Polly, with an agreeable Letter to read from Jack the Giant-Killer...

The book contained pictures, rhymes and games. Newberry's characters and imaginary authors included Woglog the Giant, Tommy Trip, Giles Gingerbread, Nurse Truelove, Peregrine Puzzlebrains, Primrose Prettyface and many others with names similar to those found in the comic-papers of our own century.

Newberry was also the originator of the 'Amazing Free Offer', so much a part of American comics. At the beginning of 1755, he had this to offer:

> Nurse Truelove's New Year Gift, or the Book of Books for children, adorned with cuts and designed as a present for every little boy who would become a great man and ride upon a fine horse; and to every little girl who would become a great woman and ride in a Lord Mayor's gilt coach. Printed for the author, who has ordered these books to be given gratis to all little boys in St. Paul's churchyard, they paying for the binding, which is only two pence each book.

Many of today's comics are crude and, like many television serials, violent in their appeal. But I did not know American comics until I was twelve, and by then I had become quite discriminating. Superman, Bulletman, Batman, Green Lantern, and other superheroes all left me cold. I had, by then, passed into the world of real books but the weakness for the comic-strip remains. I no longer receive comics in my Christmas stocking; but I do place a few in the stockings of Gautam and Siddharth. And, needless to say, I read them right through beforehand.

A MURDER IN MUSSOORIE

Conan Doyle, the creator of Sherlock Holmes, had a lifelong interest in unusual criminal cases, and his friends often passed on to him interesting accounts of crime and detection from around the world. It was in this way that he learnt of the strange death of Miss Frances Garnett-Orme in the Indian hill station of Mussoorie. Here was a murder combining the weird borders of the occult with a crime mystery as inexplicable as any devised by Doyle himself.

In April 1912 (shortly before the Titanic went down), Conan Doyle received a letter from his Sussex neighbour Rudyard Kipling:

Dear Doyle,

There has been a murder in India... A murder by suggestion at Mussoorie, which is one of the most curious things in its line on record.

Everything that is improbable, and on the face of it impossible, is in this case.

Kipling had received details of the case from a friend working in the Allahabad *Pioneer*, a paper for which, as a young man, he had worked in the 1880s. Urging Doyle to pursue the story, Kipling concluded: 'The psychology alone is beyond description.'

Doyle was indeed interested to hear more, for India had furnished him with material in the past, as in *The Sign of Four* and several short stories. Kipling, too, had turned to crime and detection in his early stories of Strickland of the Indian Police. The two writers got together and discussed the case, which was indeed a fascinating affair.

The scene was set in Mussoorie, a popular hill station in the foothills of the Himalayas. It wasn't as grand as Simla (where the Viceroy and his entourage went) but it was a charming and convivial place, with a number of hotels and boarding houses, a small military cantonment and several private schools for European children.

It was during the summer 'season' of 1911 that Miss Frances Garnett-Orme came to stay in Mussoorie, taking a suite at the Savoy, a popular resort hotel. On 28 July, she celebrated her 49th birthday. She was the daughter of George Garnett-Orme, of Skipton-in-Craven in Yorkshire, a district registrar of the Country Court. It was a family important enough to be counted among the landed gentry. Her father had died in 1892.

She came out to India in 1893 with the intention of marrying Jack Grant of the United Provinces Police. But he died in 1894 and she went back to England. Upset by his death following so soon after her father's, she turned to spiritualism in the hope of communicating with him. We must remember that spiritualism was all the rage in the early years of the century, seances and table-rappings being part of the social scene both in England and India. Madam Blavatsky, the chief exponent of spiritualism, was probably at the height of her popularity around this time; she spent her 'seasons' in neighbouring Simla, where she had many followers.

Miss Garnett-Orme's life was unsettled. She was drawn back to India, returning in 1901 to live in Lucknow, the regional capital of the United Provinces. She was still in contact with Jack Grant's family and saw his brother occasionally. The summer of 1907 was spent at Naini Tal, a hill station popular with Lucknow residents. It was here that she met Miss Eva Mountstephen, who was working as a governess.

Eva Mountstephen, too, had an interest in spiritualism. It appears that she had actually told several of her friends about this time that she had learnt (in the course of a séance) that in 1911 she would come into a great deal of money.

We are told that there was something sinister about Miss Mountstephen. She specialized in crystal-gazing, and what she saw in the glass often took a violent form. Her 'control', that is her connection in the spirit world, was a dead friend named Mrs Winter.

As a result of their common interest in the occult, Miss Garnett-Orme took on the younger woman as a companion when she returned to Lucknow in the winter. There they settled down together. But the summers were spent at one of the various hill stations. Was there a latent attraction in their relationship? It was a restless, rootless life, but they were held together by the strong and heady influence of the séance table and the crystal ball. Miss Garnett-Orme's indifferent health also made her dependent on the younger woman.

In the summer of 1911, the couple went up to Mussoorie, probably the most frivolous of hill stations, where 'seasonal' love affairs were almost the order of the day. They took rooms in the Savoy. Electricity had yet to reach Mussoorie, and it was still the age of candelabras and gas-lit streets. Every house had a grand piano. If you didn't go out to a ball, you sang or danced at home. But Miss Garnett-Orme's spiritual pursuits took precedence over these more mundane entertainments. Towards the end of the 'season', on 12 September, Miss Mountstephen returned to Lucknow to pack up their household for a move to Jhansi, where they planned to spend the winter.

On the morning of 19 September, while Miss Mountstephen

was still away, Miss Garnett-Orme was found dead in her bed. The door was locked from the inside. On her bedside table was a glass. She was positioned on the bed as though laid out by a nurse or undertaker.

Because of these puzzling circumstances, Major Birdwood of the Indian Medical Service (who was the civil surgeon in Mussoorie) was called in. He decided to hold an autopsy. It was discovered that Miss Garnett-Orme had been poisoned with prussic acid.

Prussic acid is a quick-acting poison, and would have killed too quickly for the victim to have composed herself in the way she was found. An ayah told the police that she had seen someone (she could not tell whether it was a man or a woman) slipping away through a large skylight and escaping over the roof.

Hill stations are hotbeds of rumour and intrigue, and of course, the gossips had a field day. Miss Garnett-Orme suffered from dyspepsia and was always dosing herself from a large bottle of sodium bicarbonate, which was regularly refilled. It was alleged that the bottle had been tampered with, that an unknown white powder had been added. Her doctor was questioned thoroughly. They even questioned a touring mind-reader, Mr Alfred Capper, who claimed that Miss Mountstephen had hurried from the room rather than have her mind read!

After several weeks, the police arrested Miss Mountstephen. Although she had a convincing alibi (due to her absence in Jhansi) the police sought to prove that some kind of sinister influence had been exerted on Miss Garnett-Orme to take her medicine at a particular time. Thus, through suggestion, the murderer could kill and yet be away at the time of death. In Miss Christie's first novel, *The Mysterious Affair at Styles* (1920), the poisoner was in a distant place by the time her victim reached the fatal dose; the poison having precipitated to the bottom of the mixture. Perhaps Miss Christie read accounts of the Garnett-Orme case in the British press. Even the motive was similar.

But there was no Hercule Poirot in Mussoorie, and in court, this theory could never be made convincing. The police case was never strong (they would have done better to have followed the ayah's lead), and it appears that they only acted because there was considerable ill-feeling in Mussoorie against Miss Mountstephen.

When the trial came up at Allahabad in March 1912, it caused a sensation. Murder by remote-control was something new in the annals of crime. But after hearing many days of evidence about the ladies' way of life, about crystal-gazing and premonitions of death, the court found Miss Mountstephen innocent. The Chief Justice, in delivering his verdict, remarked that the true circumstances of Miss Garnett-Orme's death would probably never be known. And he was right.

Miss Mountstephen applied for probate of her friend's will. But the Garnett-Orme family in England sent out her brother, Mr Hunter Garnett-Orme, to contest it. The case went in favour of Mr Garnett-Orme. The District Judge (W.D. Burkitt) turned down Miss Mountstephen's application on grounds of 'fraud and undue influence in connection with spiritualism and crystal-gazing'. She went in appeal to the Allahabad High Court, but the Lower Court's decision was upheld.

Miss Mountstephen returned to England. We do not know her state of mind, but if she was innocent, she must have been a deeply embittered woman. Miss Garnett-Orme's doctor lost his flourishing practice in Mussoorie and left the country too. There were rumours that he and Miss Mountstephen had conspired to get hold of Miss Garnett-Orme's considerable fortune.

There was one more puzzling feature of the case. Mr Charles Jackson, a painter friend of many of those involved, had died suddenly, apparently of cholera, two months after Miss Garnett-Orme's mysterious death. The police took an interest in his sudden demise. When he was exhumed on 23 December, the body was found to be in a perfect state of preservation. He had died of arsenic poisoning.

Murder or suicide? This puzzle, too, was never resolved. Was there a connection with Miss Garnett-Orme's death? That too we shall never know. Had Conan Doyle taken up Kipling's suggestion and involved himself in the case (as he had done in so many others in England), perhaps the outcome would have been different.

As it is, we can only make our own conjectures.

TIME STOPS AT SHAMLI

The Dehra Express usually drew into Shamli at about five o'clock in the morning, at which time the station would be dimly lit and the jungle across the tracks would just be visible in the faint light of dawn. Shamli is a small station at the foot of the Siwalik hills, and the Siwaliks lie at the foot of the Himalayas, which in turn lie at the feet of God.

The station, I remember, had only one platform, an office for the stationmaster, and a waiting room. The platform boasted a tea-stall, a fruit vendor and a few stray dogs; not much else was required, because the train stopped at Shamli for only five minutes before rushing on into the forests.

Why it stopped at Shamli, I never could tell. Nobody got off the train and nobody got in. There were never any coolies on the platform. But the train would stand there a full five minutes, and the guard would blow his whistle, and presently Shamli would be left behind and forgotten...until I passed that way again...

I was paying my relations in Saharanpur an annual visit, when the night train stopped at Shamli. I was thirty-six at the time, and still single.

On this particular journey, the train came into Shamli just as I awoke from a restless sleep. The third class compartment was crowded beyond capacity, and I had been sleeping in an upright position, with my back to the lavatory door. Now someone was trying to get into the lavatory. He was obviously hardpressed for time.

'I'm sorry, brother,' I said, moving as much as I could do to one side.

He stumbled into the closet without bothering to close the door.

'Where are we now?' I asked the man sitting beside me. He was smoking a strong aromatic bidi.

'Shamli station,' he said, rubbing the palm of a large calloused hand over the frosted glass of the window.

I let the window down and stuck my head out. There was a cool breeze blowing down the platform, a breeze that whispered of autumn in the hills. As usual there was no activity, except for the fruit-vendor walking up and down the length of the train with his basket of mangoes balanced on his head. At the tea-stall, a kettle was steaming, but there was no one to mind it. I rested my forehead on the window-ledge, and let the breeze play on my temples. I had been feeling sick and giddy but there was a wild sweetness in the wind that I found soothing.

'Yes,' I said to myself, 'I wonder what happens in Shamli, behind the station walls.'

My fellow passenger offered me a bidi. He was a farmer, I think, on his way to Dehra. He had a long, untidy, sad moustache.

We had been more than five minutes at the station. I looked up and down the platform, but nobody was getting on or off the train. Presently, the guard came walking past our compartment.

'What's the delay?' I asked him.

'Some obstruction further down the line,' he said.

'Will we be here long?'

'I don't know what the trouble is. About half an hour, at the least.'

My neighbour shrugged and, throwing the remains of his

bidi out of the window, closed his eyes and immediately fell asleep. I moved restlessly in my seat, and then the man came out of the lavatory, not so urgently now, and with obvious peace of mind. I closed the door for him.

I stood up and stretched; and this stretching of my limbs seemed to set in motion a stretching of the mind, and I found myself thinking: 'I am in no hurry to get to Saharanpur, and I have always wanted to see Shamli, behind the station walls. If I get down now, I can spend the day here, it will be better than sitting in this train for another hour. Then in the evening I can catch the next train home.'

In those days, I never had the patience to wait for second thoughts, and so I began pulling my small suitcase out from under the seat.

The farmer woke up and asked, 'What are you doing, brother?'

'I'm getting out,' I said.

He went to sleep again.

It would have taken at least fifteen minutes to reach the door, as people and their belongings cluttered up the passage; so I let my suitcase down from the window and followed it on to the platform.

There was no one to collect my ticket at the barrier, because there was obviously no point in keeping a man there to collect tickets from passengers who never came; and anyway, I had a through-ticket to my destination, which I would need in the evening.

I went out of the station and came to Shamli.

◆

Outside the station there was a neem tree, and under it stood a tonga. The tonga-pony was nibbling at the grass at the foot of the tree. The youth in the front seat was the only human in sight; there were no signs of inhabitants or habitation. I approached the tonga, and the youth stared at me as though he couldn't believe his eyes.

'Where is Shamli?' I asked.

'Why, friend, this is Shamli,' he said.

I looked around again, but couldn't see any signs of life. A dusty road led past the station and disappeared in the forest.

'Does anyone live here?' I asked.

'I live here,' he said, with an engaging smile. He looked an amiable, happy-go-lucky fellow. He wore a cotton tunic and dirty white pyjamas.

'Where?' I asked.

'In my tonga, of course,' he said. 'I have had this pony five years now. I carry supplies to the hotel. But today the manager has not come to collect them. You are going to the hotel? I will take you.'

'Oh, so there's a hotel?'

'Well, friend, it is called that. And there are a few houses too, and some shops, but they are all about a mile from the station. If they were not a mile from here, I would be out of business.'

I felt relieved, but I still had the feeling of having walked into a town consisting of one station, one pony and one man.

'You can take me,' I said. 'I'm staying till this evening.'

He heaved my suitcase into the seat beside him, and I climbed in at the back. He flicked the reins and slapped his pony on the buttocks; and, with a roll and a lurch, the buggy moved off down the dusty forest road.

'What brings you here?' asked the youth.

'Nothing,' I said. 'The train was delayed, I was feeling bored, and so I got off.'

He did not believe that; but he didn't question me further. The sun was reaching up over the forest, but the road lay in the shadow of tall trees, eucalyptus, mango and neem.

'Not many people stay in the hotel,' he said. 'So it is cheap. You will get a room for five rupees.'

'Who is the manager?'

'Mr Satish Dayal. It is his father's property. Satish Dayal could not pass his exams or get a job, so his father sent him here to look after the hotel.'

The jungle thinned out, and we passed a temple, a mosque, a few small shops. There was a strong smell of burnt sugar in the air, and in the distance I saw a factory chimney: that, then, was the reason for Shamli's existence. We passed a bullock-cart laden with sugarcane. The road went through fields of cane and maize and then, just as we were about to re-enter the jungle, the youth pulled his horse to a side road and the hotel came in sight.

It was a small white bungalow, with a garden in the front, banana trees at the sides and an orchard of guava trees at the back. We came jingling up to the front verandah. Nobody appeared, nor was there any sign of life on the premises.

'They are all asleep,' said the youth.

I said, 'I'll sit in the verandah and wait.' I got down from the tonga, and the youth dropped my case on the verandah steps. Then he stood in front of me, smiling amiably, waiting to be paid.

'Well, how much?' I asked.

'As a friend, only one rupee.'

'That's too much,' I complained. 'This is not Delhi.'

'This is Shamli,' he said. 'I am the only tonga-driver in Shamli. You may not pay me anything, if that is your wish. But then, I will not take you back to the station this evening, you will have to walk.'

I gave him the rupee. He had both charm and cunning, an effective combination.

'Come in the evening at about six,' I said.

'I will come,' he said, with an infectious smile, 'Don't worry.'

I waited till the tonga had gone round the bend in the road before walking up the verandah steps.

The doors of the house were closed, and there were no bells to ring. I didn't have a watch, but I judged the time to be a little past six o'clock. The hotel didn't look very impressive; the whitewash was coming off the walls, and the cane-chairs on the verandah were old and crooked. A stag's head was mounted over the front door, but one of its glass eyes had fallen out. I had often heard hunters speak of how beautiful an animal looked before it died, but how could anyone with a true love of the beautiful care for the stuffed head of an animal, grotesquely mounted, with no resemblance to its living aspect?

I felt too restless to take any of the chairs. I began pacing up and down the verandah, wondering if I should start banging on the doors. Perhaps the hotel was deserted; perhaps the tonga-driver had played a trick on me. I began to regret my impulsiveness in leaving the train. When I saw the manager I would have to invent a reason for coming to his hotel. I was good at inventing reasons. I would tell him that a friend of mine had stayed here some years ago, and that I was trying to trace him. I decided that my friend would have to be a little eccentric (having chosen Shamli to live in), that he had become a recluse, shutting himself off from the world; his parents—no, his sister—for his parents would be dead—had asked me to find him if I could; and, as he had last been heard of in Shamli, I had taken the opportunity to enquire after him. His name would be Major Roberts, retired.

I heard a tap running at the side of the building, and walking around, found a young man bathing at the tap. He was strong and well-built, and slapped himself on the body with great enthusiasm. He had not seen me approaching, and I waited until he had finished bathing and had began to dry himself.

'Hullo,' I said.

He turned at the sound of my voice, and looked at me for a few moments with a puzzled expression; he had a round, cheerful face and crisp black hair. He smiled slowly, but it was a more genuine smile than the tonga-driver's. So far I had met two people in Shamli, and they were both smilers; that should have cheered me, but it didn't. 'You have come to stay?' he asked, in a slow easy-going voice.

'Just for the day,' I said. 'You work here?'

'Yes, my name is Daya Ram. The manager is asleep just now, but I will find a room for you.'

He pulled on his vest and pyjamas, and accompanied me back to the verandah. Here he picked up my suitcase and, unlocking a side door, led me into the house. We went down a passageway; then Daya Ram stopped at the door on the right, pushed it open, and took me into a small, sunny room that had a window looking out on the orchard. There was a bed, a desk, a couple of cane-chairs, and a frayed and faded red carpet.

'Is it alright?' asked Daya Ram.

'Perfectly alright.'

'They have breakfast at eight o'clock. But if you are hungry, I will make something for you now.'

'No, it's alright. Are you the cook too?'

'I do everything here.'

'Do you like it?'

'No,' he said, and then added, in a sudden burst of confidence, 'There are no women for a man like me.'

'Why don't you leave, then?'

'I will,' he said, with a doubtful look on his face. 'I will leave...'

After he had gone I shut the door and went into the bathroom to bathe. The cold water refreshed me and made me feel one with the world. After I had dried myself, I sat on the bed, in front of the open window. A cool breeze, smelling of rain, came through the window and played over my body. I thought I saw a movement among the trees.

And getting closer to the window, I saw a girl on a swing. She was a small girl, all by herself, and she was swinging to and fro and singing, and her song carried faintly on the breeze.

I dressed quickly, and left my room. The girl's dress was billowing in the breeze, her pigtails flying about. When she saw me approaching, she stopped swinging, and stared at me. I stopped a little distance away.

'Who are you?' she asked.

'A ghost,' I replied.

'You look like one,' she said.

I decided to take this as a compliment, as I was determined to make friends. I did not smile at her, because some children dislike adults who smile at them all the time.

'What's your name?' I asked.

'Kiran,' she said, 'I'm ten.'

'You are getting old.'

'Well, we all have to grow old one day. Aren't you coming any closer?'

'May I?' I asked.

'You may. You can push the swing.'

One pigtail lay across the girl's chest; the other behind her shoulder. She had a serious face, and obviously felt she had responsibilities; she seemed to be in a hurry to grow up, and I suppose she had no time for anyone who treated her as a child. I pushed the swing, until it went higher and higher, and then I stopped pushing, so that she came lower each time and we could talk.

'Tell me about the people who live here,' I said.

'There is Heera,' she said. 'He's the gardener. He's nearly a hundred. You can see him behind the hedges in the garden. You can't see him unless you look hard. He tells me stories—a new story every day. He's much better than the people in the hotel, and so is Daya Ram.'

'Yes, I met Daya Ram.'

'He's my bodyguard. He brings me nice things from the kitchen when no one is looking.'

'You don't stay here?'

'No, I live in another house; you can't see it from here. My father is the manager of the factory.'

'Aren't there any other children to play with?' I asked.

'I don't know any,' she said.

'And the people staying here?'

'Oh, they.' Apparently Kiran didn't think much of the hotel guests. 'Miss Deeds is funny when she's drunk. And Mr Lin is the strangest.'

'And what about the manager, Mr Dayal?'

'He's mean. And he gets frightened of slightest things. But Mrs Dayal is nice; she lets me take flowers home. But she doesn't talk much.'

I was fascinated by Kiran's ruthless summing up of the guests. I brought the swing to a standstill and asked, 'And what do you think of me?'

'I don't know as yet,' said Kiran quite seriously. 'I'll think about you.'

◆

As I came back to the hotel, I heard the sound of a piano in one of the front rooms. I didn't know enough about music to be able to recognize the piece, but it had sweetness and melody, though it was played with some hesitancy. As I came nearer, the sweetness deserted the music, probably because the piano was out of tune.

The person at the piano had distinctive Mongolian features, and so I presumed he was Mr Lin. He hadn't seen me enter the room, and I stood beside the curtains of the door, watching him play. He had full round lips and high, slanting cheekbones. His eyes were large and round and full of melancholy. His long, slender fingers hardly touched the keys.

I came nearer; and then he looked up at me, without any show of surprise or displeasure, and kept on playing.

'What are you playing?' I asked.

'Chopin,' he said.

'Oh, yes. It's nice, but the piano is fighting it.'

'I know. This piano belonged to one of Kipling's aunts. It hasn't been tuned since the last century.'

'Do you live here?'

'No, I come from Calcutta,' he answered readily. 'I have some business here with the sugarcane people actually, though I am not a businessman.' He was playing softly all the time, so that our conversation was not lost in the music. 'I don't know anything about business. But I have to do something.'

'Where did you learn to play the piano?'

'In Singapore. A French lady taught me. She had great hopes of my becoming a concert pianist when I grew up. I would have toured Europe and America.'

'Why didn't you?'

'We left during the war, and I had to give up my lessons.'

'And why did you go to Calcutta?'

'My father is a Calcutta businessman. What do you do, and why do you come here?' he asked. 'If I am not being too inquisitive.'

Before I could answer, a bell rang, loud and continuously, drowning the music and conversation.

'Breakfast,' said Mr Lin.

A thin dark man, wearing glasses, stepped nervously into the room and peered at me in an anxious manner.

'You arrived last night?'

'That's right,' I said, 'I just want to stay the day. I think you're the manager?'

'Yes. Would you like to sign the register?'

I went with him past the bar and into the office. I wrote my name and Mussoorie address in the register, and the duration of my stay. I paused at the column marked 'Profession', thought it would be best to fill it with something and wrote 'Author'.

'You are here on business?' asked Mr Dayal.

'No, not exactly. You see, I'm looking for a friend of mine who was heard of in Shamli, about three years ago. I thought I'd make a few enquiries in case he's still here.'

'What was his name? Perhaps he stayed here.'

'Major Roberts,' I said. 'An Anglo-Indian.'

'Well, you can look through the old registers after breakfast.'

He accompanied me into the dining-room. The establishment was really more of a boarding house than a hotel, because Mr Dayal ate with his guests. There was a round mahogany dining-table in the centre of the room, and Mr Lin was the only one seated at it. Daya Ram hovered about with plates and trays. I took my seat next to Lin, and, as I did so, a door opened from the passage, and a woman of about thirty-five came in.

She had on a skirt and blouse, which accentuated a firm, well-rounded figure, and she walked on high-heels, with a rhythmical swaying of the hips. She had an uninteresting face, camouflaged with lipstick, rouge and powder—the powder so thick that is had become embedded in the natural lines of her face—but her figure compelled admiration.

'Miss Deeds,' whispered Lin.

There was a false note to her greeting.

'Hallo, everyone,' she said heartily, straining for effect. 'Why are you all so quiet? Has Mr Lin been playing the Funeral March again?' She sat down and continued talking. 'Really, we must have a dance or something to liven things up. You must know some good numbers Lin, after your experience in Singapore night-clubs. What's for breakfast? Boiled eggs. Daya Ram, can't you make an omelette for a change? I know you're not a professional cook, but you don't have to give us the same thing every day, and there's absolutely no reason why you should burn the toast. You'll have to do something about a cook, Mr Dayal.' Then she noticed me sitting opposite her. 'Oh, hallo,' she said, genuinely surprised. She gave me a long appraising look.

'This gentleman,' said Mr Dayal introducing me, 'is an author.'

'That's nice,' said Miss Deeds. 'Are you married?'

'No,' I said. 'Are you?'

'Funny, isn't it,' she said, without taking offence, 'No one in this house seems to be married.'

'I'm married,' said Mr Dayal.

'Oh, yes, of course,' said Miss Deeds. 'And what brings you to Shamli?' she asked, turning to me.

'I'm looking for a friend called Major Roberts.'

Lin gave an exclamation of surprise. I thought he had seen through my deception.

But another game had begun.

'I knew him,' said Lin. 'A great friend of mine.'

◆

'Yes,' continued Lin. 'I knew him. A good chap, Major Roberts.'

Well, there I was, inventing people to suit my convenience, and people like Mr Lin started inventing relationships with them. I was too intrigued to try and discourage him. I wanted to see how far he would go.

'When did you meet him?' asked Lin, taking the initiative.

'Oh, only about three years back. Just before he disappeared. He was last heard of in Shamli.'

'Yes, I heard he was here,' said Lin. 'But he went away, when he thought his relatives had traced him. He went into the mountains near Tibet.'

'Did he?' I said, unwilling to be instructed further. 'What part of the country? I come from the hills myself. I know the Mana and Niti passes quite well. If you have any idea of exactly where he went. I think I could find him.' I had the advantage in this exchange, because I was the one who had originally invented Roberts. Yet I couldn't bring myself to end his deception, probably because I felt sorry for him. A happy man wouldn't take the trouble of inventing friendships with people who didn't exist; he'd be too busy with friends who did.

'You've had a lonely life, Mr Lin?' I asked.

'Lonely?' said Mr Lin, with forced incredulousness. 'I'd never been lonely till I came here a month ago. When I was in Singapore—'

'You never get any letters though, do you?' asked Miss Deeds suddenly.

Lin was silent for a moment. Then he said, 'Do you?'

Miss Deeds lifted her head a little, as a horse does when it is annoyed, and I thought her pride had been hurt; but then she laughed unobstrusively and tossed her head.

'I never write letters,' she said. 'My friends gave me up as hopeless years ago. They know it's no use writing to me, because they rarely get a reply. They call me the Jungle Princess.'

Mr Dayal tittered, and I found it hard to suppress a smile. To cover up my smile I asked, 'You teach here?'

'Yes, I teach at the girl's school,' she said with a frown. 'But don't talk to me about teaching. I have enough of it all day.'

'You don't like teaching?'

She gave an aggressive look. 'Should I?' she asked.

'Shouldn't you?' I said.

She paused, and then said, 'Who are you, anyway, the Inspector of Schools?'

'No,' said Mr Dayal who wasn't following very well. 'He's a journalist.'

'I've heard they are nosey,' said Miss Deeds.

Once again Lin interrupted to steer the conversation away from a delicate issue.

'Where's Mrs Dayal this morning?' asked Lin.

'She spent the night with our neighbours,' said Mr Dayal. 'She should be here after lunch.'

It was the first time Mrs Dayal had been mentioned. Nobody spoke either well or ill of her; I suspected that she kept her distance from the others, avoiding familiarity. I began to wonder about Mrs Dayal.

◆

Daya Ram came in from the verandah, looking worried.

'Heera's dog has disappeared,' he said. 'He thinks a leopard took it.'

Heera, the gardener was standing respectfully outside on the verandah steps. We all hurried out to him, firing questions which he didn't try to answer.

'Yes. It's a leopard,' said Kiran, appearing from behind Heera.
'It's going to come into the hotel,' she added cheerfully.

'Be quiet,' said Satish Dayal crossly.

'There are pug marks under the trees,' said Daya Ram.

Mr Dayal, who seemed to know little about leopards or pug
marks, said, 'I will take a look,' and led the way to the orchard,
the rest of us trailing behind in an ill-assorted procession.

There were marks on the soft earth in the orchard (they
could have been a leopard's), which went in the direction of
the riverbed. Mr Dayal paled a little and went hurrying back to
the hotel. Heera returned to the front garden, the least excited,
the most sorrowful. Everyone else was thinking of a leopard,
but he was thinking of the dog.

I followed him, and watched him weeding the sunflower
beds. His face wrinkled like a walnut, but his eyes were clear and
bright. His hands were thin and bony, but there was a deftness
and power in the wrist and fingers, and the weeds flew fast from
his spade. He had cracked, parchment-like skin. I could not help
thinking of the gloss and glow of Daya Ram's limbs, as I had
seen them when he was bathing, and wondered if Heera's had
once been like that and if Daya Ram's would ever be like this,
and both possibilities—or were they probabilities?—saddened
me. Our skin, I thought, is like the leaf of a tree, young and
green and shiny; then it gets darker and heavier, sometimes
spotted with disease, sometimes eaten away; then fading, yellow
and red, then falling, crumbling into dust or feeding the flames
of fire. I looked at my own skin, still smooth, not coarsened by
labour; I thought of Kiran's fresh rose-tinted complexion; Miss
Deed's skin, hard and dry; Lin's pale taut skin, stretched tightly
across his prominent cheeks and forehead; and Mr Dayal' s grey
skin, growing thick hair. And I wondered about Mrs Dayal and
the kind of skin she would have.

'Did you have the dog for long?' I asked Heera.

He looked up with surprise, for he had been unaware of my presence.

'Six years, sahib,' he said. 'He was not a clever dog, but he was very friendly. He followed me home one day, when I was coming back from the bazaar. I kept telling him to go away, but he wouldn't. It was a long walk and so I began talking to him. I liked talking to him, and I have always talked with him, and we have understood each other. That first night, when I came home, I shut the gate between us. But he stood on the other side, looking at me with trusting eyes. Why did he have to look at me like that?'

'So, you kept him?'

'Yes, I could never forget the way he looked at me. I shall feel lonely now, because he was my only companion. My wife and son died long ago. It seems I am to stay here forever, until everyone has gone, until there are only ghosts in Shamli. Already the ghosts are here...'

I heard a light footfall behind me and turned to find Kiran. The bare-footed girl stood beside the gardener, and with her toes, began to pull at the weeds.

'You are a lazy one,' said the old man. 'If you want to help me, sit down and use your hands.'

I looked at the girl's fair round face, and in her bright eyes I saw something old and wise; and I looked into the old man's wise eyes, and saw something forever bright and young. The skin cannot change the eyes; the eyes are the true reflection of a man's age and sensibilities; even a blind man has hidden eyes.

'I hope we shall find the dog,' said Kiran. 'But I would like a leopard. Nothing ever happens here.'

'Not now,' sighed Heera. 'Not now... Why, once there was a band and people danced till morning, but now...'

'I have always been here,' said Heera. 'I was here before Shamli.'

'Before the station?'

'Before there was a station, or a factory, or a bazaar. It was a village then, and the only way to get here was by bullock-cart. Then a bus service was started, then the railway lines were laid and a station built, then they started the sugar factory, and for a few years Shamli was a town. But the jungle was bigger than the town. The rains were heavy and malaria was everywhere. People didn't stay long in Shamli. Gradually, they went back into the hills. Sometimes I too want to go back to the hills, but what is the use when you are old and have no one left in the world except a few flowers in a troublesome garden. I had to choose between the flowers and the hills, and I chose the flowers. I am tired now, and old, but I am not tired of flowers.'

I could see that his real world was the garden; there was more variety in his flower-beds than there was in the town of Shamli. Every month, every day, there were new flowers in the garden, but there were always the same people in Shamli.

I left Kiran with the old man, and returned to my room. It must have been about eleven o'clock.

◆

I was facing the window when I heard my door being opened. Turning, I perceived the barrel of a gun moving slowly round the edge of the door. Behind the gun was Satish Dayal, looking hot and sweaty. I didn't know what his intentions were; so, deciding it would be better to act first and reason later, I grabbed a pillow from the bed and flung it in his face. I then threw myself at his legs and brought him crashing down to the ground.

When we got up, I was holding the gun. It was an old

Enfield rifle, probably dating back to the Afghan wars; the kind that goes off at the least encouragment.

'But—but—why?' stammered the dishevelled and alarmed Mr Dayal.

'I don't know,' I said menacingly. 'Why did you come in here pointing this at me?'

'I wasn't pointing it at you. It's for the leopard.'

'Oh, so you came into my room looking for a leopard? You have, I presume, been stalking one about the hotel?' (By now I was convinced that Mr Dayal had taken leave of his senses and was hunting imaginary leopards.)

'No, no,' cried the distraught man, becoming more confused, 'I was looking for you. I wanted to ask you if you could use a gun. I was thinking we should go looking for the leopard that took Heera's dog. Neither Mr Lin nor I can shoot.'

'Your gun is not up-to-date.' I said. 'It's not at all suitable for hunting leopards. A stout stick would be more effective. Why don't we arm ourselves with lathis and make a general assault?'

I said this banteringly, but Mr Dayal took the idea quite seriously. 'Yes, yes,' he said with alacrity, 'Daya Ram has got one or two lathis in the godown. The three of us could make an expedition. I have asked Mr Lin but he says he doesn't want to have anything to do with leopards.'

'What about our Jungle Princess?' I said. 'Miss Deeds should be pretty good with a lathi.'

'Yes, yes,' said Mr Dayal humourlessly, 'but we'd better not ask her.'

Collecting Daya Ram and two lathis, we set off for the orchard and began following the pug marks through the trees. It took us ten minutes to reach the riverbed, a dry hot rocky place; then we went into the jungle, Mr Dayal keeping well to the rear. The atmosphere was heavy and humid, and there was not a breath of air amongst the trees. When a parrot squawked suddenly, shattering the silence, Mr Dayal let out a startled exclamation and started for home.

'What was that?' he asked nervously.

'A bird,' I explained.

'I think we should go back now,' he said, 'I don't think the leopard's here.'

'You never know with leopards,' I said, 'They could be anywhere.'

Mr Dayal stepped away from the bushes. 'I'll have to go,' he said. 'I have a lot of work. You keep a lathi with you, and I'll send Daya Ram back later.'

'That's very thoughtful of you,' I said.

Daya Ram scratched his head and reluctantly followed his employer back through the trees. I moved on slowly down the little-used path, wondering if I should also return. I saw two monkeys playing on the branch of a tree, and decided that there could be no danger in the immediate vicinity.

Presently, I came to a clearing where there was a pool of fresh clear water. It was fed by a small stream that came suddenly, like a snake, out of the long grass. The water looked cool and inviting; laying down the lathi and taking off my clothes, I ran down the bank until I was waist-deep in the middle of the pool. I splashed about for some time, before emerging; then I lay on the soft grass and allowed the sun to dry my body. I closed my eyes and gave myself up to beautiful thoughts. I had forgotten all about leopards.

I must have slept for about half an hour because when I awoke, I found that Daya Ram had come back and was vigorously thrashing about in the narrow confines of the pool. I sat up and asked him the time.

'Twelve o'clock,' he shouted, coming out of water, his

dripping body all gold and silver in sunlight. 'They will be waiting for dinner.'

'Let them wait,' I said.

It was a relief to talk to Daya Ram, after the uneasy conversations in the lounge and dining-room.

'Dayal sahib will be angry with me.'

'I'll tell him we found the trail of the leopard, and that we went so far into the jungle that we lost our way. As Miss Deeds is so critical of the food, let her cook the meal.'

'Oh, she only talks like that,' said Daya Ram. 'Inside she is very soft. She is too soft in some ways.'

'She should be married.'

'Well, she would like to be. Only there is no one to marry her. When she came here she was engaged to be married to an English army captain; I think she loved him, but she is the sort of person who cannot help loving many men all at once, and the captain could not understand that—it is just the way she is made, I suppose. She is always ready to fall in love.'

'You seem to know,' I said.

'Oh, yes.'

We dressed and walked back to the hotel. In a few hours, I thought, the tonga will come for me and I will be back at the station; the mysterious charm of Shamli will be no more, but whenever I pass this way I will wonder about these people, about Miss Deeds and Lin and Mrs Dayal.

Mrs Dayal... She was the one person I was yet to meet; it was with some excitement and curiosity that I looked forward to meeting her; she was about the only mystery left to Shamli, now, and perhaps she would be no mystery when I met her. And yet... I felt that perhaps she would justify the impulse that made me get down from the train.

I could have asked Daya Ram about Mrs Dayal, and so

satisfied my curiosity; but I wanted to discover her for myself. Half the day was left to me, and I didn't want my game to finish too early.

I walked towards the verandah, and the sound of the piano came through the open door.

'I wish Mr Lin would play something cheerful,' said Miss Deeds. 'He's obsessed with the Funeral March. Do you dance?'

'Oh no,' I said.

She looked disappointed. But when Lin left the piano, she went into the lounge and sat down on the stool. I stood at the door watching her, wondering what she would do.

Lin left the room, somewhat resentfully.

She began to play an old song, which I remembered having heard in a film or on a gramophone record. She sang while she played, in a slightly harsh but pleasant voice:

Rolling round the world
Looking for the sunshine
I know I'm going to find some day...

Then she played *Am I blue?* and *Darling, Je Vous Aime Beaucoup.* She sat there singing in a deep husky voice, her eyes a little misty, her hard face suddenly kind and sloppy. When the gong rang, she broke off playing, and shook off her sentimental mood, and laughed derisively at herself.

I don't remember that lunch. I hadn't slept much since the previous night and I was beginning to feel the strain of my journey. The swim had refreshed me, but it had also made me drowsy. I ate quite well, though, of rice and kofta curry, and then, feeling sleepy, made for the garden to find a shady tree.

There were some books on the shelf in the lounge, and I ran my eye over them in search of one that might condition sleep. But they were too dull to do even that. So I went into the garden, and there was Kiran on the swing, and I went to her tree and sat down on the grass.

'Did you find the leopard?' she asked.

'No,' I said, with a yawn.

'Tell me a story.'

'You tell me one,' I said.

'Alright. Once there was a lazy man with long legs, who was always yawning and wanting to fall asleep...'

I watched the swaying motions of the swing and the movements of the girl's bare legs, and a tiny insect kept buzzing about in front of my nose... 'and fall asleep, and the reason for this was that he liked to dream.' I blew the insect away, and the swing became hazy and distant, and Kiran was a blurred figure in the trees...

'...liked to dream, and what do you think he dreamt about...?' Dreamt about, dreamt about...

◆

When I awoke there was that cool rain-scented breeze blowing across the garden. I remember lying on the grass with my eyes closed, listening to the swishing of the swing. Either I had not slept long, or Kiran had been a long time on the swing; it was moving slowly now, in a more leisurely fashion, without much sound. I opened my eyes and saw that my arm was stained with the juice of the grass beneath me. Looking up, I expected to see Kiran's legs waving above me. But instead I saw dark slim feet, and above them the folds of a sari. I straightened up against the trunk of the tree to look closer at Kiran, but Kiran wasn't there, it was someone else on the swing, a young woman in a pink sari and with a red rose in her hair.

She had stopped the swing with her foot on the ground, and she was smiling at me.

It wasn't a smile you could see, it was a tender fleeting movement that came suddenly and was gone at the same time, and its going was sad. I thought of the others' smiles, just as I had thought of their skins: the tonga-driver's friendly, deceptive grin; Daya Ram's wide sincere smile; Miss Deed's cynical, derisive smile. And looking at Sushila, I knew a smile could never change. She had always smiled that way.

'You haven't changed,' she said.

I was standing up now, though still leaning against the tree for support. Though I had never thought much about the *sound* of her voice, it seemed as familiar as the sounds of yesterday.

'You haven't changed either,' I said. 'But where did you come from?' I wasn't sure yet if I was awake or dreaming.

She laughed, as she had always laughed at me.

'I came from behind the tree. The little girl has gone.'

'Yes, I'm dreaming,' I said helplessly.

'But what brings you here?'

'I don't know. At least I didn't know when I came. But it must have been you. The train stopped at Shamli, and I don't know why, but I decided I would spend the day here, behind the station walls. You must be married now, Sushila.'

'Yes, I am married to Mr Dayal, the manager of the hotel. And what has been happening with you?'

'I am still a writer, still poor, and still living in Mussoorie.'

'When were you last in Delhi?' she asked. 'I don't mean Delhi, I mean at home.'

'I have not been to your home since you were there.'

'Oh, my friend,' she said, getting up suddenly and coming to me, 'I want to talk to you. I want to talk about our home and Sunil and our friends and all those things that are so far away now. I have been here two years, and I am already feeling old. I keep remembering our home, how young I was, how happy, and I am all alone with memories. But now *you* are here! It was a bit of magic, I came through the trees after Kiran had gone, and there you were, fast asleep under the tree. I didn't wake you then, because I wanted to see you wake up.'

'As I used to watch you wake up...'

She was near me and I could look at her more closely. Her cheeks did not have the same freshness; they were a little pale, and she was thinned now, but her eyes were the same, smiling the same way. Her voice was the same. Her fingers, when she took my hand, were the same warm delicate fingers.

'Talk to me,' she said. 'Tell me about yourself.'

'You tell me,' I said.

'I am here,' she said. 'That is all there is about myself.'

'Then let us sit down and I'll talk.'

'Not here.' She took my hand and led me through the trees. 'Come with me.'

I heard the jingle of a tonga-bell and a faint shout; I stopped and laughed.

'My tonga,' I said. 'It has come to take me back to the station.'

'But you are not going,' said Sushila, immediately downcast.

'I will tell him to come in the morning,' I said. 'I will spend the night in your Shamli.'

I walked to the front of the hotel where the tonga was waiting. I was glad no one else was in sight. The youth was smiling at me in his most appealing manner.

'I'm not going today,' I said. 'Will you come tomorrow morning?'

'I can come whenever you like, friend. But you will have to pay for every trip, because it is a long way from the station even if my tonga is empty.'

'Alright, how much?'

'Usual fare, friend, one rupee.'

I didn't try to argue but resignedly gave him the rupee. He cracked his whip and pulled on the reins, and the carriage moved off.

'If you don't leave tomorrow,' the youth called out after me, 'you'll never leave Shamli!'

I walked back to the trees, but I couldn't find Sushila.

'Sushila, where are you?' I called, but I might have been speaking to the trees, for I had no reply. There was a small path going through the orchard, and on the path I saw a rose petal. I walked a little further and saw another petal. They were from Sushila's red rose. I walked on down the path until I had skirted the orchard, and then the path went along the fringe of the jungle, past a clump of bamboos, and here the grass was a lush green as though it had been constantly watered. I was still finding rose petals. I heard the chatter of seven sisters, and the call of hoopoe. The path bent to meet a stream; there was a willow coming down to the water's edge, and Sushila was waiting there.

'Why didn't you wait?' I said.

'I wanted to see if you were as good at following me as you used to be.'

'Well, I am,' I said, sitting down beside her on the grassy bank of the stream. 'Even if I'm out of practice.'

'Yes, I remember the time you climbed onto an apple tree to pick some fruit for me. You got up alright but then you couldn't come down again. I had to climb up myself and help you.'

'I don't remember that,' I said.

'Of course you do.'

'It must have been your other friend, Pramod.'

'I never climbed trees with Pramod.'

'Well, I don't remember.'

I looked at the little stream that ran past us. The water was no more than ankle-deep, cold and clear and sparkling, like the mountain-stream near my home. I took off my shoes, rolled up my trousers and put my feet in water. Sushila's feet joined mine.

At first I had wanted to ask her about her marriage, whether she was happy or not, what she thought of her husband; but now I couldn't ask her these things, they seemed far away and of little importance. I could think of nothing she had in common with Mr Dayal; I felt that her charm and attractiveness and warmth could not have been appreciated, or even noticed, by that curiously distracted man. He was much older than her, of course; probably older than me; he was obviously not her choice but her parents'; and so far they were childless. Had there been children, I don't think Sushila would have minded Mr Dayal as her husband. Children would have made up for the absence of passion—or was there passion in Satish Dayal? I remembered having heard that Sushila had been married to a man she didn't like; I remembered having shrugged off the news, because it meant she would never come my way again, and I have never yearned after something that has been irredeemably lost. But she had come my way again. And was she still lost? That was what I wanted to know...

'What do you do with yourself all day?' I asked.

'Oh, I visit the school and help with the classes. It is the only interest I have in this place. The hotel is terrible. I try to keep away from it as much as I can.'

'And what about the guests?'

'Oh, don't let us talk about them. Let us talk about ourselves. Do you have to go tomorrow?'

'Yes, I suppose so. Will you always be in this place?'

'I suppose so.'

That made me silent. I took her hand, and my feet churned

up the mud at the bottom of the stream. As the mud subsided, I saw Sushila's face reflected in the water; and looking up at her again, into her dark eyes, the old yearning returned and I wanted to care for her and protect her, I wanted to take her away from that place, from sorrowful Shamli; I wanted her to live again. Of course, I had forgotten all about my poor finances, Sushila's family, and the shoes I wore, which were my last pair. The uplift I was experiencing in this meeting with Sushila, who had always, throughout her childhood and youth, bewitched me as no other had ever bewitched me, made me reckless and impulsive.

I lifted her hand to my lips and kissed her in the soft of the palm.

'Can I kiss you?' I said.

'You have just done so.'

'Can I kiss you?' I repeated.

'It is not necessary.'

I leaned over and kissed her slender neck. I knew she would like this, because that was where I had kissed her often before. I kissed her in the soft of the throat, where it tickled.

'It is not necessary,' she said, but she ran her fingers through my hair and let them rest there. I kissed her behind the ear then, and kept my mouth to her ear and whispered, 'Can I kiss you?'

She turned her face to me so that we were deep in each other's eyes, and I kissed her again, and we put our arms around each other and lay together on the grass, with the water running over our feet; and we said nothing at all, simply lay there for what seemed like several years, or until the first drop of rain.

It was a big wet drop, and it splashed on Sushila's cheek, just next to mine, and ran down to her lips, so that I had to kiss her again. The next big drop splattered on the tip of my nose, and Sushila laughed and sat up. Little ringlets were forming on the stream where the raindrops hit the water, and above us there was a pattering on the banana leaves.

'We must go,' said Sushila.

We started homewards, but had not gone far before it was raining steadily, and Sushila's hair came loose and streamed down her body. The rain fell harder, and we had to hop over pools and avoid the soft mud. Sushila's sari was plastered to her body, accentuating her ripe, thrusting breasts, and I was excited to passion, and pulled her beneath a big tree and crushed her in my arms and kissed her rain-kissed mouth. And then I thought she was crying, but I wasn't sure, because it might have been the raindrops on her cheeks.

'Come away with me,' I said. 'Leave this place. Come away with me tomorrow morning. We will go somewhere where nobody will know us or come between us.'

She smiled at me and said, 'You are still a dreamer, aren't you?'

'Why can't you come?'

'I am married; it is as simple as that.'

'If it is that simple, you can come.'

'I have to think of my parents, too. It would break my father's heart if I were to do what you are proposing. And you are proposing it without a thought for the consequences.'

'You are too practical,' I said.

'If women were not practical, most marriages would be failures.'

'So, your marriage is a success?'

'Of course it is, as a marriage. I am not happy and I do not love him, but neither am I so unhappy that I should hate him. Sometimes, for our own sakes, we have to think of the happiness of others. What happiness would we have living in hiding from everyone we once knew and cared for? Don't be a fool. I am always here and you can come to see me, and nobody will be made unhappy by it. But take me away and we will only have regrets.'

'You don't love me,' I said foolishly.

'That sad word love,' she said, and became pensive and silent.

I could say no more. I was angry again, and rebellious, and there was no one and nothing to rebel against. I could not understand someone who was afraid to break away from an unhappy existence lest that existence should become unhappier; I had always considered it an admirable thing to break away from security and respectability. Of course it is easier for a man to do this, a man can look after himself, he can do without neighbours and the approval of the local society. A woman, I reasoned, would do anything for love provided it was not at the price of security; for a woman loves security as much as a man loves independence.

'I must go back now,' said Sushila. 'You follow a little later.'

'All you wanted to do was talk,' I complained.

She laughed at that, and pulled me playfully by the hair; then she ran out from under the tree, springing across the grass, and the wet mud flew up and flecked her legs. I watched her through the thin curtain of rain, until she reached the verandah. She turned to wave to me, and then skipped into the hotel. She was still young; but I was no younger.

◆

The rain had lessened, but I didn't know what to do with myself. The hotel was uninviting, and it was too late to leave Shamli. If the grass hadn't been wet I would have preferred to sleep under a tree rather than return to the hotel to sit at that alarming dining-table.

I came out from under the trees and crossed the garden. But instead of making for the verandah I went round to the back of the hotel. Smoke issuing from the barred window of a back room told me I had probably found the kitchen. Daya Ram was inside, squatting in front of a stove, stirring a pot of stew. The stew smelt appetizing. Daya Ram looked up and smiled at me.

'I thought you must have gone,' he said.

'I'll go in the morning,' I said, pulling myself upon an empty table. Then I had one of my sudden ideas and said, 'Why don't you come with me? I can find you a good job in Mussoorie. How much do you get paid here?'

'Fifty rupees a month. But I haven't been paid for three months.'

'Could you get your pay before tomorrow morning?'

'No, I won't get anything until one of the guests pays a bill. Miss Deeds owes about fifty rupees on whisky alone. She will pay up, she says, when the school pays her salary. And the school can't pay her until they collect the children's fees. That is how bankrupt everyone is in Shamli.'

'I see,' I said, though I didn't see. 'But Mr Dayal can't hold back your pay just because his guests haven't paid their bills.'

'He can, if he hasn't got any money.'

'I see,' I said, 'Anyway, I will give you my address. You can come when you are free.'

'I will take it from the register,' he said.

I edged over to the stove and, leaning over, sniffed at the stew. 'I'll eat mine now,' I said; and without giving Daya Ram a chance to object, I lifted a plate off the shelf, took hold of the stirring-spoon and helped myself from the pot.

'There's rice too,' said Daya Ram.

I filled another plate with rice and then got busy with my fingers. After ten minutes, I had finished. I sat back comfortably in the hotel, in ruminative mood. With my stomach full I could take a more tolerant view of life and people. I could understand Sushila's apprehensions, Lin's delicate lying and Miss Deed's aggressiveness. Daya Ram went out to sound the dinner-gong, and I trailed back to my room.

From the window of my room I saw Kiran running across the lawn, and I called to her, but she didn't hear me. She ran down the path and out of the gate, her pigtails beating against the wind.

The clouds were breaking and coming together again, twisting and spiralling their way across a violet sky. The sun was going down behind the Siwaliks. The sky there was blood-shot. The tall slim trunks of the eucalyptus tree were tinged with an orange glow; the rain had stopped, and the wind was a soft, sullen puff, drifting sadly through the trees. There was a steady drip of water from the eaves of the roof on to the window-sill. Then the sun went down behind the old, old hills, and I remembered my own hills, far beyond these.

The room was dark but I did not turn on the light. I stood near the window, listening to the garden. There was a frog warbling somewhere, and there was a sudden flap of wings overhead. Tomorrow morning I would go, and perhaps I would come back to Shamli one day, and perhaps not; I could always come here looking for Major Roberts, and, who knows, one day I might find him. What should he be like, this lost man? A romantic, a man with a dream, a man with brown skin and blue eyes, living in a hut on a snowy mountain-top, chopping wood and catching fish and swimming in cold mountain streams; a rough, free man with a kind heart and a shaggy beard, a man who owed allegiance to no one, who gave a damn for money and politics and cities and civilizations, who was his own master, who lived at one with nature knowing no fear. But that was not Major Roberts—that was the man I wanted to be. He was not a Frenchman or an Englishman, he was me, a dream of myself. If only I could find Major Roberts.

When Daya Ram knocked on the door and told me the others had finished dinner, I left my room and made for the lounge. It was quite lively in the lounge. Satish Dayal was at the bar, Lin at the piano, and Miss Deeds in the centre of the room, executing a tango on her own. It was obvious she had been drinking heavily.

'All on credit,' complained Mr Dayal to me. 'I don't know when I'll be paid, but I don't dare to refuse her anything for fear she starts breaking up the hotel.'

'She could do that, too,' I said. 'It comes down without much encouragement.'

Lin began to play a waltz (I think it was waltz), and then I found Miss Deeds in front of me, saying 'Wouldn't you like to dance, old boy?'

'Thank you,' I said, somewhat alarmed. 'I hardly know how to.'

'Oh, come on, be a sport,' she said, pulling me away from the bar. I was glad Sushila wasn't present; she wouldn't have minded, but she'd have laughed as she always laughed when I made a fool of myself.

We went round the floor in what I suppose was waltz-time, though all I did was mark time to Miss Deeds' motions; we were not very steady—this was because I was trying to keep her at arm's length, whilst she was determined to have me crushed to her bosom. At length, Lin finished the waltz. Giving him a grateful look, I pulled myself free. Miss Deeds went over to the piano, leant right across it, and said, 'Play some lively, dear Mr Lin, play some hot stuff.'

To my surprise, Mr Lin, without so much as an expression of distaste or amusement, began to execute what I suppose was the frug or the jitterbug. I was glad she hadn't asked me to dance that one with her.

It all appeared very incongruous to me: Miss Deeds letting herself go in crazy abandonment, Lin playing the piano with great seriousness and Mr Dayal watching from the bar with an anxious frown. I wondered what Sushila would have thought of them now.

Eventually, Miss Deeds collapsed on the couch breathing heavily. 'Give me a drink,' she cried.

With the noblest of intentions I took her a glass of water. Miss Deeds took a sip and made a face. 'What's this stuff?' she asked. 'It is different.'

'Water,' I said.

'No,' she said, 'now don't joke, tell me what it is.'

'It's water, I assure you,' I said.

When she saw that I was serious, her face coloured up, and I thought she would throw the water at me; but she was too tired to do this, and contented herself by throwing the glass over her shoulder. Mr Dayal made a dive for the flying glass, but he wasn't in time to rescue it, and it hit the wall and fell to pieces on the floor.

Mr Dayal wrung his hands. 'You'd better take her to her room,' he said, as though I were personally responsible for her behaviour just because I'd danced with her.

'I can't carry her alone,' I said, making an unsuccessful attempt at helping Miss Deeds up from the couch.

Mr Dayal called for Daya Ram, and the big amiable youth came lumbering into the lounge. We took an arm each and helped Miss Deeds, feet dragging, across the room. We got her to her room and on to her bed. When we were about to withdraw she said, 'Don't go, my dear, stay with me a little while.'

Daya Ram had discreetly slipped outside. With my hand

on the doorknob I said, 'Which of us?'

'Oh, are there two of you?' said Miss Deeds, without a trace of disappointment.

'Yes, Daya Ram helped me carry you here.'

'Oh, and who are you?'

'I'm the writer. You danced with me, remember?'

'Of course. You dance divinely, Mr Writer. Do stay with me. Daya Ram can stay too if he likes.'

I hesitated, my hand on the doorknob. She hadn't opened her eyes all the time I'd been in the room, her arms hung loose, and one bare leg hung over the side of the bed. She was fascinating somehow, and desirable, but I was afraid of her. I went out of the room and quietly closed the door.

◆

As I lay awake in bed I heard the jackal's 'pheau', the cry of fear, which it communicates to all the jungle when there is danger about, a leopard or a tiger. It was a weird howl, and between each note there was a kind of low gurgling. I switched off the light and peered through the closed window. I saw the jackal at the edge of the lawn. It sat almost vertically on its haunches, holding its head straight up to the sky, making the neighbourhood vibrate with the eerie violence of its cries. Then suddenly it started up and ran off into the trees.

Before getting back into bed I made sure the window was fast. The bull-frog was singing again, 'ing-ong; ing-ong', in some foreign language. I wondered if Sushila was awake too, thinking about me. It must have been almost eleven o'clock. I thought of Miss Deeds, with her leg hanging over the edge of the bed. I tossed restlessly, and then sat up. I hadn't slept for two nights but I was not sleepy. I got out of bed without turning on the light and, slowly opening my door, crept down the passageway. I stopped at the door of Miss Deed's room. I stood there listening, but I heard only the ticking of the big clock that might have been in the room or somewhere in the passage. I put my hand on the doorknob, but the door was bolted. That settled the matter.

I would definitely leave Shamli the next morning. Another day in the company of these people and I would be behaving like them. Perhaps I was already doing so! I remembered the tonga-driver's words, 'Don't stay too long in Shamli or you will never leave!'

When the rain came, it was not with a preliminary patter or shower, but all at once, sweeping across the forest like a massive wall, and I could hear it in the trees long before it reached the house. Then it came crashing down on the corrugated roofing, and the hailstones hit the window panes with a hard metallic sound, so that I thought the glass would break. The sound of thunder was like the booming of big guns, and the lightning kept playing over the garden. At every flash of lightning I sighted the swing under the tree, rocking and leaping in the air as though some invisible, agitated being was sitting on it. I wondered about Kiran. Was she sleeping through all this, blissfully unconcerned, or was she lying awake in bed, starting at every clash of thunder, as I was; or was she up and about, exulting in the storm? I half expected to see her come running through the trees, through the rain, to stand on the swing with her hair blowing wild in the wind, laughing at the thunder and the angry skies. Perhaps I did see her, perhaps she was there. I wouldn't have been surprised if she were some forest nymph, living in the hole of a tree, coming out sometimes to play in the garden.

A crash, nearer and louder than any thunder so far, made me sit up in the bed with a start. Perhaps lightning had struck the house. I turned on the switch, but the light didn't come on. A tree must have fallen across the line.

I heard voices in the passage, the voices of several people. I stepped outside to find out what had happened, and started at the appearance of a ghostly apparition right in front of me; it was Mr Dayal standing on the threshold in an oversized pyjama suit, a candle in his hand.

'I came to wake you,' he said. 'This storm.'

He had the irritating habit of stating the obvious.

'Yes, the storm,' I said. 'Why is everybody up?'

'The back wall has collapsed and part of the roof has fallen in. We'd better spend the night in the lounge, it is the safest room. This is a very old building,' he added apologetically.

'Alright,' I said. 'I am coming.'

The lounge was lit by two candles; one stood over the piano, the other on a small table near the couch. Miss Deeds was on the couch, Lin was at the piano-stool, looking as though he would start playing Stravinsky any moment, and Mr Dayal was fussing about the room. Sushila was standing at a window, looking out at the stormy night. I went to the window and touched her, She didn't look round or say anything. The lightning flashed and her dark eyes were pools of smouldering fire.

'What time will you be leaving?' she said.

'The tonga will come for me at seven.'

'If I come,' she said. 'If I come with you, I will be at the station before the train leaves.'

'How will you get there?' I asked, and hope and excitement rushed over me again.

'I will get there,' she said. 'I will get there before you. But if I am not there, then do not wait, do not come back for me. Go on your way. It will mean I do not want to come. Or I will be there.'

'But are you sure?'

'Don't stand near me now. Don't speak to me unless you have to.' She squeezed my fingers, then drew her hand away. I sauntered over to the next window, then back into the centre of the room. A gust of wind blew through a cracked window-pane and put out the candle near the couch.

'Damn the wind,' said Miss Deeds.

♦

The window in my room had burst open during the night, and there were leaves and branches strewn about the floor. I sat down on the damp bed, and smelt eucalyptus. The earth was red, as though the storm had bled it all night.

After a little while, I went into the verandah with my suitcase, to wait for the tonga. It was then that I saw Kiran under the trees. Kiran's long black pigtails were tied up in a red ribbon, and she looked fresh and clean like the rain and the red earth. She stood looking seriously at me.

'Did you like the storm?' she asked.

'Some of the time,' I said. 'I'm going soon. Can I do anything for you?'

'Where are you going?'

'I'm going to the end of the world. I'm looking for Major Roberts, have you seen him anywhere?'

'There is no Major Roberts,' she said perceptively. 'Can I come with you to the end of the world?'

'What about your parents?'

'Oh, we won't take them.'

'They might be annoyed if you go off on your own.'

'I can stay on my own. I can go anywhere.'

'Well, one day I'll come back here and I'll take you everywhere and no one will stop us. Now is there anything else I can do for you?'

'I want some flowers, but I can't reach them,' she pointed to a hibiscus tree that grew against the wall. It meant climbing the wall to reach the flowers. Some of the red flowers had fallen during the night and were floating in a pool of water.

'Alright,' I said and pulled myself up on the wall. I smiled down into Kiran's serious upturned face. 'I'll throw them to you and you can catch them.'

I bent a branch, but the wood was young and green, and I had to twist it several times before it snapped.

'I hope nobody minds,' I said, as I dropped the flowering branch to Kiran.

'It's nobody's tree,' she said.

'Sure?'

She nodded vigorously. 'Sure, don't worry.'

I was working for her and she felt immensely capable of protecting me. Talking and being with Kiran, I felt a nostalgic longing for the childhood: emotions that had been beautiful because they were never completely understood.

'Who is your best friend?' I said.

'Daya Ram,' she replied. 'I told you so before.'

She was certainly faithful to her friends.

'And who is the second best?'

She put her finger in her mouth to consider the question; her head dropped sideways in concentration.

'I'll make you the second best,' she said.

I dropped the flowers over her head. 'That is so kind of you. I'm proud to be your second best.'

I heard the tonga bell, and from my perch on the wall saw the carriage coming down the driveway. 'That's for me,' I said. 'I must go now.'

I jumped down the wall. And the sole of my shoe came off at last.

'I knew that would happen,' I said.

'Who cares for shoes,' said Kiran.

'Who cares,' I said.

I walked back to the verandah, and Kiran walked beside me, and stood in front of the hotel while I put my suitcase in the tonga.

'You nearly stayed one day too late,' said the tonga-driver. 'Half the hotel has come down, and tonight the other half will come down.'

I climbed into the back seat. Kiran stood on the path, gazing intently at me.

'I'll see you again,' I said.

'I'll see you in Iceland or Japan,' she said. 'I'm going everywhere.'

'Maybe,' I said, 'maybe you will.'

We smiled, knowing and understanding each other's importance. In her bright eyes I saw something old and wise. The tonga-driver cracked his whip, the wheels cracked, the carriage rattled down the path. We kept waving to each other. In Kiran's hand was a spring of hibiscus. As she waved, the blossoms fell apart and danced a little in the breeze.

◆

Shamli station looked the same as it had the day before. The same train stood at the same platform, and the same dogs prowled beside the fence. I waited on the platform until the bell clanged for the train to leave, but Sushila did not come.

Somehow, I was not disappointed. I had never really expected her to come. Unattainable, Sushila would always be more bewitching and beautiful than if she were mine.

Shamli would always be there. And I could always come back, looking for Major Roberts.

THE LAST TONGA RIDE

It was a warm spring day in Dehra, and the walls of the bungalow were aflame with flowering bougainvillaea. The papayas were ripening. The scent of sweetpeas drifted across the garden. Grandmother sat in an easy chair in a shady corner of the verandah, her knitting needles clicking away, her head nodding now and then. She was knitting a pullover for my father. 'Delhi has cold winters,' she had said; and although the winter was still eight months away, she had set to work on getting our woollens ready.

In the Kathiawar states, touched by the warm waters of the Arabian Sea, it had never been cold but Dehra lies at the foot of the first range of the Himalayas.

Grandmother's hair was white, her eyes were not very strong but her fingers moved quickly with the needles and the needles kept clicking all morning.

When Grandmother wasn't looking, I picked geranium leaves, crushed them between my fingers and pressed them to my nose.

I had been in Dehra with my grandmother for almost a month and I had not seen my father during this time. We had never before been separated for so long. He wrote to me every week, and sent me books and picture postcards; and I would walk to the end of the road to meet the postman as early as possible, to see if there was any mail for us.

We heard the jingle of tonga-bells at the gate, and a familiar horse-buggy came rattling up the drive.

'I'll see who's come,' I said, and ran down the verandah steps and across the garden.

It was Bansi Lal in his tonga. There were many tongas and tonga-drivers in Dehra but Bansi was my favourite driver. He was young and handsome and he always wore a clean white shirt and pyjamas. His pony, too, was bigger and faster than the other tonga ponies. Bansi didn't have a passenger, so I asked him, 'What have you come for, Bansi?'

'Your grandmother sent for me, dost.' He did not call me 'chota sahib' or 'baba', but 'dost' and this made me feel much more important. Not every small boy could boast of a tonga-driver for his friend!

'Where are you going, Granny?' I asked, after I had run back to the verandah.

'I'm going to the bank.'

'Can I come too?'

'Whatever for? What will you do in the bank?'

'Oh, I won't come inside, I'll sit in the tonga with Bansi.'

'Come along, then.'

We helped Grandmother into the back seat of the tonga, and then I joined Bansi in the driver's seat. He said something to his pony, and the pony set off at a brisk trot, out of the gate and down the road.

'Now, not too fast, Bansi,' said Grandmother, who didn't like anything that went too fast—tonga, motor car, train or bullock-cart.

'Fast?' said Bansi. 'Have no fear, Memsahib. This pony has never gone fast in its life. Even if a bomb went off behind us, we could go no faster. I have another pony, which I use for racing when customers are in a hurry. This pony is reserved for you, Memsahib.'

There was no other pony, but Grandmother did not know this, and was mollified by the assurance that she was riding in the slowest tonga in Dehra.

A ten-minute ride brought us to the bazaar. Grandmother's bank, the Allahabad Bank, stood near the clock tower. She was gone for about half an hour and during this period Bansi and I sauntered about in front of the shops. The pony had been left with some green stuff to munch.

'Do you have any money on you?' asked Bansi.

'Four annas,' I said.

'Just enough for two cups of tea,' said Bansi, putting his arm round my shoulders and guiding me towards a tea stall. The money passed from my palm to his.

'You can have tea, if you like,' I said. 'I'll have a lemonade.'

'So be it, friend. A tea and a lemonade, and be quick about it,' said Bansi to the boy in the stall and presently the drinks were set before us and Bansi was making a sound rather like his pony when he drank, while I burped my way through some green, gaseous stuff that tasted more like soap than lemonade.

When Grandmother came out of the bank, she looked pensive, and did not talk much during the ride back to the house except to tell me to behave myself when I leaned over to pat the pony on its rump. After paying off Bansi, she marched straight indoors.

'When will you come again?' I asked Bansi.

'When my services are required, dost. I have to make a living, you know. But I tell you what, since we are friends, the next time I am passing this way after leaving a fare, I will jingle my bells at the gate and if you are free and would like a ride—a fast ride—you can join me. It won't cost you anything. Just bring some money for a cup of tea.'

'All right—since we are friends,' I said.

'Since we are friends.'

And touching the pony very lightly with the handle of his whip, he sent the tonga rattling up the drive and out of the gate. I could hear Bansi singing as the pony cantered down the road.

Ayah was waiting for me in the bedroom, her hands resting on her broad hips—sure sign of an approaching storm.

'So you went off to the bazaar without telling me,' she said. (It wasn't enough that I had Grandmother's permission!) 'And all this time I've been waiting to give you your bath.'

'It's too late now, isn't it?' I asked hopefully.

'No, it isn't. There's still an hour left for lunch. Off with your clothes!'

While I undressed, Ayah berated me for keeping the company of tonga-drivers like Bansi. I think she was a little jealous.

'He is a rogue, that man. He drinks, gambles and smokes opium. He has TB and other terrible diseases. So don't you be too friendly with him, understand, baba?'

I nodded my head sagely but said nothing. I thought Ayah was exaggerating, as she always did about people, and besides, I had no intention of giving up free tonga rides.

As my father had told me, Dehra was a good place for trees, and Grandmother's house was surrounded by several kinds— peepul, seem, mango, jackfruit, papaya and an ancient banyan tree. Some of the trees had been planted by my father and grandfather.

'How old is the jackfruit tree?' I asked Grandmother.

'Now let me see,' said Grandmother, looking very thoughtful. 'I should remember the jackfruit tree. Oh yes, your grandfather put it down in 1927. It was during the rainy season. I remember, because it was your father's birthday and we celebrated it by planting a tree. 14 July 1927. Long before you were born!'

The banyan tree grew behind the house. Its spreading branches, which hung to the ground and took root again, formed a number of twisting passageways in which I liked to wander. The tree was older than the house, older than my grandparents, as old as Dehra. I could hide myself in its branches behind thick, green leaves and spy on the world below.

It was an enormous tree, about sixty feet high, and the first time I saw it I trembled with excitement because I had never seen such a marvellous tree before. I approached it slowly, even cautiously, as I wasn't sure the tree wanted my friendship. It looked as though it had many secrets. There were sounds and movement in the branches but I couldn't see who or what made the sounds.

The tree made the first move, the first overture of friendship. It allowed a leaf to fall.

The leaf brushed against my face as it floated down, but before it could reach the ground I caught and held it. I studied the leaf, running my fingers over its smooth, glossy texture. Then I put out my hand and touched the rough bark of the tree and this felt good to me. So I removed my shoes and socks as people do when they enter a holy place; and finding first a foothold and then a handhold on that broad trunk, I pulled myself up with the help of the tree's aerial roots.

As I climbed, it seemed as though someone was helping me; invisible hands, the hands of the spirit in the tree, touched me and helped me climb.

But although the tree wanted me, there were others who were disturbed and alarmed by my arrival. A pair of parrots suddenly shot out of a hole in the trunk and, with shrill cries, flew across the garden—flashes of green and red and gold. A squirrel looked out from behind a branch, saw me, and went scurrying away to inform his friends and relatives.

I climbed higher, looked up, and saw a red beak poised above my head. I shrank away, but the hornbill made no attempt to attack me. He was relaxing in his home, which was a great hole in the tree trunk. Only the bird's head and great beak were showing. He looked at me in a rather bored way, drowsily opening and shutting his eyes.

'So many creatures live here,' I said to myself. 'I hope none of them are dangerous!'

At that moment, the hornbill lunged at a passing cricket. Bill and tree trunk met with a loud and resonant 'Tonk!'

I was so startled that I nearly fell out of the tree. But it was a difficult tree to fall out of! It was full of places where one could sit or even lie down. So I moved away from the hornbill, crawled along a branch that had sent out supports, and so moved quite a distance from the main body of the tree. I left its cold, dark depths for an area penetrated by shafts of sunlight.

No one could see me. I lay flat on the broad branch hidden by a screen of leaves. People passed by on the road below. A sahib in a sun-helmet. His memsahib twirling a coloured silk sun-umbrella. Obviously she did not want to get too brown and be mistaken for a country-born person. Behind them, a pram wheeled along by a nanny.

Then there were a number of Indians; some in white dhotis, some in western clothes, some in loincloths. Some with baskets on their heads. Others with coolies to carry their baskets for them.

A cloud of dust, the blare of a horn, and down the road, like an out-of-condition dragon, came the latest Morris touring car. Then cyclists. Then a man with a basket of papayas balanced on his head. Following him, a man with a performing monkey. This man rattled a little hand drum, and children followed the man and the monkey along the road. They stopped in the shade of a mango tree on the other side of the road. The little red monkey wore a frilled dress and a baby's bonnet. It danced for the children, while the man sang and played his drum.

The clip-clop of a tonga pony, and Bansi's tonga came rattling down the road. I called down to him and he reined in with a shout of surprise, and looked up into the branches of the banyan tree.

'What are you doing up there?' he cried.

'Hiding from Grandmother,' I said.

'And when are you coming for that ride?'

'On Tuesday afternoon,' I said.

'Why not today?'

'Ayah won't let me. But she has Tuesdays off.'

Bansi spat red paan juice across the road. 'Your ayah is jealous,' he said.

'I know,' I said. 'Women are always jealous, aren't they? I suppose it's because she doesn't have a tonga.'

'It's because she doesn't have a tonga-driver,' said Bansi, grinning up at me. 'Never mind. I'll come on Tuesday—that's the day after tomorrow, isn't it?'

I nodded down to him, and then started backing along my branch, because I could hear Ayah calling in the distance. Bansi leant forward and smacked his pony across the rump, and the tonga shot forward.

'What were you doing up there?' asked Ayah a little later.

'I was watching a snake cross the road,' I said. I knew she couldn't resist talking about snakes. There weren't as many in Dehra as there had been in Kathiawar and she was thrilled that I had seen one.

'Was it moving towards you or away from you?' she asked.

'It was going away.'

Ayah's face clouded over. 'That means poverty for the beholder,' she said gloomily.

Later, while scrubbing me down in the bathroom, she began to air all her prejudices, which included drunkards ('they die quickly anyway'), misers ('they get murdered sooner or later') and tonga-drivers ('they have all the vices').

'You are a very lucky boy,' she said suddenly, peering closely at my tummy.

'Why?' I asked. 'You just said I would be poor because I saw a snake going the wrong way.'

'Well, you won't be poor for long. You have a mole on your tummy, and that's very lucky. And there is one under your armpit, which means you will be famous. Do you have one on the neck? No, thank God! A mole on the neck is the sign of a murderer!'

'Do you have any moles?' I asked.

Ayah nodded seriously, and pulling her sleeve up to her shoulder, showed me a large mole high on her arm.

'What does that mean?' I asked.

'It means a life of great sadness,' said Ayah gloomily.

'Can I touch it?' I asked.

'Yes, touch it,' she said, and taking my hand, she placed it against the mole.

'It's a nice mole,' I said, wanting to make Ayah happy. 'Can I kiss it?'

'You can kiss it,' said Ayah.

I kissed her on the mole.

'That's nice,' she said.

Tuesday afternoon came at last, and as soon as Grandmother was asleep and Ayah had gone to the bazaar, I was at the gate, looking up and down the road for Bansi and his tonga. He was not long in coming. Before the tonga turned into the road,

I could hear his voice, singing to the accompaniment of the carriage bells. He reached down, took my hand, and hoisted me on to the seat beside him. Then we went off down the road at a steady jogtrot. It was only when we reached the outskirts of the town that Bansi encouraged his pony to greater efforts. He rose in his seat, leaned forward and slapped the pony across the haunches. From a brisk trot we changed to a carefree canter. The tonga swayed from side to side. I clung to Bansi's free arm, while he grinned at me, his mouth red with paan juice.

'Where shall we go, dost?' he asked.

'Nowhere,' I said. 'Anywhere.'

'We'll go to the river,' said Bansi.

The 'river' was really a swift mountain stream that ran through the forests outside Dehra, joining the Ganga about fifteen miles away. It was almost dry during the winter and early summer; in flood during the monsoon.

The road out of Dehra was a gentle decline and soon we were rushing headlong through the tea gardens and eucalyptus forests, the pony's hoofs striking sparks off the metalled road, the carriage wheels groaning and creaking so loudly that I feared one of them would come off and that we would all be thrown into a ditch or into the small canal that ran beside the road. We swept through mango groves, through guava and litchi orchards, past broad-leaved sal and shisham trees. Once in the sal forest, Bansi turned the tonga on to a rough cart track, and we continued along it for about a furlong, until the road dipped down to the stream bed.

'Let us go straight into the water,' said Bansi. 'You and I and the pony!' And he drove the tonga straight into the middle of the stream, where the water came up to the pony's knees.

'I am not a great one for baths,' said Bansi, 'but the pony needs one, and why should a horse smell sweeter than its owner?' Saying which, he flung off his clothes and jumped into the water.

'Better than bathing under a tap!' he cried, slapping himself on the chest and thighs. 'Come down, dost, and join me!'

After some hesitation I joined him, but had some difficulty in keeping on my feet in the fast current. I grabbed at the pony's tail, and hung on to it, while Bansi began sloshing water over the patient animal's back.

After this, Bansi led both me and the pony out of the stream and together we gave the carriage a good washing down. I'd had a free ride and Bansi got the services of a free helper for the long overdue spring cleaning of his tonga. After we had finished the job, he presented me with a packet of aam pafiat—a sticky toffee made from mango pulp—and for some time I tore at it as a dog tears at a hit of old leather. Then I felt drowsy and lay down on the brown, sun-warmed grass. Crickets and grasshoppers were telephoning each other from tree and bush and a pair of bluejays rolled, dived and swooped acrobatically overhead.

Bansi had no watch. He looked at the sun and said, 'It is past three. When will that ayah of yours be home? She is more frightening than your grandmother!'

'She comes at four.'

'Then we must hurry back. And don't tell her where we've been, or I'll never be able to come to your house again. Your grandmother's one of my best customers.'

'That means you'd be sorry if she died.'

'I would indeed, my friend.'

Bansi raced the tonga back to town. There was very little motor traffic in those days, and tongas and bullock-carts were far more numerous than they are today.

We were back five minutes before Ayah returned. Before

Bansi left, he promised to take me for another ride the following week.

◆

The house in Dehra had to be sold. My father had not left any money; he had never realized that his health would deteriorate so rapidly from the malarial fevers which had grown in frequency; he was still planning for the future when he died. Now that my father had gone, Grandmother saw no point in staying on in India; there was nothing left in the bank and she needed money for our passages to England, so the house had to go. Dr Ghose, who had a thriving medical practice in Dehra, made her a reasonable offer, which she accepted.

Then things happened very quickly. Grandmother sold most of our belongings, because as she said, we wouldn't be able to cope with a lot of luggage. The kabaris came in droves, buying our crockery, furniture, carpets and clocks at throwaway prices. Grandmother hated parting with some of her possessions, such as the carved giltwood mirror, her walnut-wood armchair and her rosewood writing desk, but it was impossible to take them with us. They were carried away in a bullock-cart.

Ayah was very unhappy at first but cheered up when Grandmother got her a job with a tea-planter's family in Assam. It was arranged that she could stay with us until we left Dehra.

We left at the end of September, just as the monsoon clouds broke up, scattered, and were driven away by soft breezes from the Himalayas. There was no time to revisit the island where my father and I had planted our trees. And in the urgency and excitement of the preparations for our departure, I forgot to recover my small treasures from the hole in the banyan tree. It was only when we were in Bansi's tonga, on the way to the station, that I remembered my top, catapult and Iron Cross.

Too late! To go back for them would mean missing the train.

'Hurry!' urged Grandmother nervously. 'We mustn't be late for the train, Bansi.'

Bansi flicked the reins and shouted to his pony, and for once in her life Grandmother submitted to being carried along the road at a brisk trot.

'It's five to nine,' she said, 'and the train leaves at nine.'

'Do not worry, Memsahib. I have been taking you to the station for fifteen years, and you have never missed a train!'

'No,' said Grandmother. 'And I don't suppose you'll ever take me to the station again, Bansi.'

'Times are changing, Memsahib. Do you know that there is now a taxi—a *motor car*—competing with the tongas of Dehra? You are lucky to be leaving. If you stay, you will see me starve to death!'

'We will all starve to death if we don't catch that train,' said Grandmother.

'Do not worry about the train, it never leaves on time, and no one expects it to. If it left at nine o' clock, everyone would miss it.'

Bansi was right. We arrived at the station at five minutes past nine, and rushed on to the platform, only to find that the train had not yet arrived.

The platform was crowded with people waiting to catch the same train or to meet people arriving on it. Ayah was there already, standing guard over a pile of miscellaneous luggage. We sat down on our boxes and became part of the platform life at an Indian railway station.

Moving among piles of bedding and luggage were sweating, cursing coolies; vendors of magazines, sweetmeats, tea and betel-leaf preparations; also stray dogs, stray people and sometimes a stray stationmaster. The cries of the vendors mixed with the general clamour of the station and the shunting of a steam engine in the yards. 'Tea, hot tea!' Sweets, papads, hot stuff, cold drinks, toothpowder, pictures of film stars, bananas, balloons, wooden toys, clay images of the gods. The platform had become a bazaar.

Ayah was giving me all sorts of warnings.

'Remember, baba, don't lean out of the window when the train is moving. There was that American boy who lost his head last year! And don't eat rubbish at every station between here and Bombay. And see that no strangers enter the compartment. Mr Wilkins was murdered *and* robbed last year!'

The station bell clanged, and in the distance there appeared a big, puffing steam engine, painted green and gold and black. A stray dog, with a lifetime's experience of trains, darted away across the railway lines. As the train came alongside the platform, doors opened, window shutters fell, faces appeared in the openings, and even before the train had come to a stop, people were trying to get in or out.

For a few moments there was chaos. The crowd surged backward and forward. No one could get out. No one could get in. A hundred people were leaving the train, two hundred were getting into it. No one wanted to give way.

The problem was solved by a man climbing out of a window. Others followed his example and the pressure at the doors eased and people started squeezing into their compartments.

Grandmother had taken the precaution of reserving berths in a first-class compartment, and assisted by Bansi and half a dozen coolies, we were soon inside with all our luggage. A whistle blasted and we were off! Bansi had to jump from the running train.

As the engine gathered speed, I ignored Ayah's advice and put my head out of the window to look back at the receding platform. Ayah and Bansi were standing on the platform, waving to me and I kept waving to them until the train rushed into the darkness and the bright lights of Dehra were swallowed up in the night. New lights, dim and flickering came into existence as we passed small villages. The stars too were visible and I saw a shooting star streaking through the heavens.

I remembered something that Ayah had once told me, that stars are the spirits of good men, and I wondered if that shooting star was a sign from my father that he was aware of our departure and would be with us on our journey. And I remembered something else that Ayah had said—that if one wished on a shooting star, one's wish would be granted, provided of course that one thrust all five fingers into the mouth at the same time!

'What on earth are you doing?' asked Grandmother staring at me as I thrust my hand into my mouth.

'Making a wish,' I said.

'Oh,' said Grandmother.

She was preoccupied, and didn't ask me what I was wishing for; nor did I tell her.

REMEMBER THE OLD ROAD

Remember the old road,
The steep stony path
That took us up from Rajpur,
Toiling and sweating
And grumbling at the climb,
But enjoying it all the same.
At first the hills were hot and bare,
But then there were trees near Jharipani
And we stopped at the Halfway House
And swallowed lungfuls of diamond-cut air.
Then onwards, upwards, to the town,
Our appetites to repair!

Well, no one uses the old road any more.
Walking is out of fashion now.
And if you have a car to take you
Swiftly up the motor road
Why bother to toil up a disused path?
You'd have to be an old romantic like me
To want to take that route again.
But I did it last year,
Pausing and plodding and gasping for air—
Both road and I being a little worse for wear!
But I made it to the top and stopped to rest

And looked down to the valley and the silver stream
Winding its way towards the plains.
And the land stretched out before me, and the years fell away,
And I was a boy again,
And the friends of my youth were there beside me,
And nothing had changed.

THE OLD SUITCASE

The autobiography of my suitcase is, in many respects, my own autobiography.

I bought it in Jersey, in the Channel Islands, in 1952, and for well over sixty-five years it has given shelter to so many of my personal effects—socks, underwear, shirts, trousers; books, notebooks, pens, paper, passport; and in recent years (when, like its owner, it is showing signs of wear and tear): a receptacle for old manuscripts, photographs, newspaper cuttings, publisher's contracts and the flotsam of a lifetime of putting pen to paper.

For the last few years the suitcase had lain under my bed, so forgotten that the mice had managed to get in, building a nest from old newspapers; and I was woken one night by the squealing of baby mice—several of them. I was about to evict the family when I remembered the times when I had been evicted from lodgings, so I allowed them a respite of several days—a sort of stay order—before tipping the lot into an empty flowerpot and hoping for the best.

The suitcase was in a sad condition, but I was loath to throw it away. You don't throw away old friends. Or do you? There are all-weather friends and there are fair-weather friends, and it can take time to tell one from the other. The old suitcase had been with one long enough to be called both friend and philosopher, and so I hung on to it.

◆

It was a very cheap suitcase—the cheapest I could find in that Woolworth's Store in Jersey, when I was eighteen and ready to try my luck in London. I had spent a year in Jersey, living with my aunt's family and working as a junior clerk in the Public Health Department. Late evening I'd sit down at my small portable typewriter (bought with the help of a loan from Mr Bromley, a kind senior clerk) and work on the novel that I was writing—the novel that was to become *The Room on the Roof*; but I was keen to move to London, where there were publishers and writers and bookshops and theatres, and I was saving something out of my weekly wage of £3 in order to make that dream a reality.

I had saved about £12 when a decision to leave was forced upon me as result of a quarrel I had with my uncle, a good man but somewhat set in his way of thinking.

I used to keep a diary at the time, and I'd made the mistake of leaving it on my desk near the typewriter in the attic room where I worked. My uncle, prowling around while I was out at work, had come across and read some entries in which I had expressed dissatisfaction with his narrow-mindedness and extreme political views. He confronted me with the diary. He accused me of being an ingrate and a 'nigger lover' (his words) and suggested that I leave his house.

So, of course, I took up his suggestion, gave a week's notice to the Public Health Department, and packed my belongings. Jersey was not for me.

But I needed a suitcase—and a cheap one. The tin trunk I had brought from India was unsuitable for travelling about in England, where you had to manage your own luggage. The suitcase I found was very light—made of some sort of reinforced hardboard—and I did not expect it to last very long. But it was big enough for my few belongings, and it cost £2 and a few shillings.

And so, with my new suitcase in my right hand, and the typewriter in my left hand, I boarded the ferry for Southampton, and eight hours later found myself on the train to London— without a job, without a home to go to, and with a half-written novel as my only asset.

◆

The gales of Jersey were exchanged for the fog of London. March is probably the most dismal month in that hardy city— fog outside, and indoors the smell of leaking gas. Continuous drizzle. Aspidistras growing in dark corners of boarding-house entrance halls. The sun a distant memory. I cursed myself for leaving India.

An old school friend put me up in his small room for almost a month. He loved cooking, and the room was always full of the fragrance of curries and spices. I found a job and a room of my own, and typewriter, suitcase and I ascended the stairs to a tiny attic room in a boarding house in Glenmore Road.

It was a depressing little room, but I was out most of the day, working in an office in distant Soho, or wandering about looking for cheap cafés, living off beans on toast or 'meat and two veg'—the staple chow in the ABC restaurants. When I had money to spare I went to the cinema. Everyone smoked in those days, and it was difficult to see the screen through the haze of smoke that drifted through the hall.

I left Glenmore Road for Haverstock Hill, my suitcase getting heavier with the few books that I had been acquiring. At night I worked on my novel—the first draft written by hand, the second draft typed out on my little portable.

Diana Athill, a partner in the firm of Andre Deutsch, and about fifteen years my senior befriended me and had me over for dinner on several occasions. She gave me an old raincoat—we were about the same height—and out of gratitude I showed her how to make a curry. I think it was more of a stew than a curry, but we managed to consume it.

Then the three friends—suitcase, typewriter and budding author—moved to Tooting, in South London.

Why Tooting?

Well, I'd fallen in love with this wonderful girl from Vietnam. She was a student and her name was Vu-Phuong, meaning 'like the wind', and true enough, she came and went like the wind.

She was sweet company, and for several weeks we spent a lot of time together—strolling in Kensington Gardens, wandering through the hothouses in Kew, even going to the opera. It was my suggestion that we go to the opera. The cheaper seats were right at the back of the huge opera house, and we couldn't hear much of the singing, not even the rollicking Toreador song (it was *Carmen*)—it was much better on gramophone records!

On a rainy day in June we joined the crowds on the streets, watching Queen Elizabeth's coach pass by in all its splendour. Vu had a pretty umbrella and I had Diana Athill's raincoat, so we did not mind the rain.

And then, unaccountably, Vu stopped seeing me. She even changed her lodgings without giving me her new address. I tried to trace her, but without any success. Then I received a note from her saying she was returning to her home in Hanoi. The Vietnam War was at its height, and Hanoi was part of Communist-held territory. It was possible that she was under pressure to avoid contact with 'Westerners'. I was no Westerner, but how were her political bosses to know that? Heartbroken, I left Tooting—how I hated Tooting!—and returned to the more familiar streets of Belsize Park.

I told Diana of my unhappy plight—I would often confide in her—and to cheer me up she took me to St Paul's Cathedral to hear Yehudi Menuhin, the great violinist, give a recital. It was a moving experience, and for once I felt grateful to London for giving me the opportunity to hear great music.

◆

Another kind of music assailed me when I made friends with a bunch of West Indians, newly arrived in England. They invited me to a calypso party in a flat in Brixton (right next to the prison), and the dancing and revelry continued till dawn. Unthinking, I invited them to hold their next party in my bedsitter (now a fairly spacious one) in Belsize Park. The party was a great success, the building shuddered to its foundations as the rum flowed and the dancing grew frenetic, and the next day my landlord gave me twenty-four-hours' notice to leave the premises.

I lugged my suitcase and typewriter down the road to Swiss Cottage, where a kindly Jewish landlady (my third Jewish landlady) took me in and gave me a pleasant room with a large window which let in the sunlight on those few occasions when the sun came out. She even gave me a good breakfast. But she warned me against having parties in the room. And no lady visitors. And no pin-ups on the walls. Down came Eartha Kitt.

I was quite happy in Swiss Cottage, but after nearly four years away from India I felt it was time to go home.

'No job for you here,' my mother had warned me. 'And you won't make any money from writing. Better stay in England.'

But I was not to be put off. Home is where the heart is, and my heart was still in the foothills of Dehra.

After much dithering, Diana and Andre Deutsch gave me a cheque for £50 as an advance against my novel, which had finally been accepted. This was the standard advance in those days. Publication was still a year off, but I did not feel like hanging around in London any longer. The fare to Bombay—by the cheapest passenger liner, the M. S. *Batory*, a Polish ship—was just under £40. I bought a ticket, gave a week's notice to my employer, thanked Diana for her many kindnesses, and bought a second suitcase.

This new suitcase cost more than the old one, and was quite flashy, but it was not to last as long. The cheap hardboard suitcase had accompanied me all over London, from one boarding house to another, and had attached itself to me like an unwanted stray, knowing no one else would keep it.

◆

The M. S. *Batory* had a reputation for being unlucky, and even before it sailed half the crew had sought political asylum in the UK. But it had a good bar, serving Polish vodka, and only one passenger fell overboard in the course of the voyage.

At Gibraltar I went ashore and bought several bottles of perfume from an Indian trader. These, I thought, would make suitable presents for friends and family. At Port Said I went ashore and had my pocket picked; fortunately I'd kept most of my money in the old suitcase. At Aden I went ashore and did nothing; there was nothing to do and nothing to see. At Bombay I stepped ashore with my suitcases and was met by a couple of young customs officials and told to open them. I did so, and they took away all my bottles of perfume. Contraband, they said.

Happy homecoming!

'What will they do with it?' I asked a fellow passenger.

'Give it all to their girlfriends this evening,' he said knowingly.

At least they left my typewriter alone. And suitcases, typewriter and I arrived in Dehradun without further mishap. I had no presents for anyone, but I was welcomed back anyway.

◆

And so began three years of freelancing, bombarding every magazine and newspaper in the land with stories, articles and anything they would publish and pay for! The little typewriter broke down from all the strain, the letter 'b' breaking off; being irreplaceable, I had to go through all my typescripts and fill in the 'b's' by hand. Stories and articles would only be considered if typed, so I had no choice but to go through with this chore, cursing all the time, the letter 'b' being most appropriate for this purpose: 'Bugger the bloody B!' In all my years of writing, I have never used swear words in print—and now here I am, doing just that!

While my typewriter was getting a battering, the suitcase was enjoying a well-earned rest. It was put to use again when I moved to Delhi for three or four years, a period when my creative efforts were at their lowest ebb. As a writer I am greatly influenced by my surroundings and environment, and the Delhi (or rather, New Delhi) of the 1960s failed to get my creative juices flowing.

There was only one thing to do—pack up, and take to the hills.

It was a wise move although not always a restful one. Landlords, leaking roofs, crumbling hillsides and water shortages all involved moving from one dwelling to another—Maplewood Lodge, Wayside Cottage (on the old Kipling Road), a flat near the Mall, then up to Landour's Prospect Point and down again to Ivy Cottage! The old suitcase was kept fairly busy, now used more as a receptacle for books and papers. The latches had rusted away and I had to use a length of rope to close the suitcase; but it held up wonderfully well, although it was just reinforced hardboard.

For several years it was located under my bed, and whenever I came across some interesting relic, by way of an old magazine or newspaper, I would store it away for reference. My collection included the *Madras Mail Annual* of 1926, an issue of *The Statesman* (1936, I think) reporting on the horrors of the Quetta earthquake and a copy of *Life* (1947) carrying a feature on the changes that were taking place in India at the time of Independence. This had a picture of me, looking very angelic, saying my prayers in the school chapel of Bishop Cotton School, Simla, referred to in the article as the 'Eton of the East'. I think I was chosen for the picture partly because I looked angelic and partly because I was one of the handful of English-looking boys left in the school. But there was nothing angelic about me when I was thirteen, just as there is nothing angelic about me now.

Over a period of time the mice had managed to gnaw their way through the fabric of the suitcase and had made a neat little home for themselves among my souvenirs. As they did no great damage, I left them alone, live and let live always having been my motto.

Then last month we had a terrible storm. The window burst open, the glass fell out, the rain came pouring into the room, and by morning the suitcase was half-full of water. The mice had already gone, but everything made of paper had been ruined and had to be thrown away.

The suitcase was put out to dry on the verandah, but it did not look as though it would recover.

'Shall I throw it away?' asked Beena, my granddaughter. 'It's falling to pieces.'

Do you throw away an old friend just because he's a cripple

and of no use to anyone any more? For over sixty-four years that cheap hardboard suitcase had been my constant companion, a witness to all my struggles, my successes, my failures, my follies.

'No, we can't throw it away,' I said, 'Put it in the attic, fill it with all those pastries I'm not supposed to eat, and let the mice make merry!'

ONCE UPON A MOUNTAIN TIME

My solitude is not my own, for I see now how much it belongs to them—and that I have a responsibility for it in their regard, not just in my own. It is because I am one with them that I owe it to them to be alone, and when I am alone they are not 'they' but my own self. There are no strangers!

From *Confessions of a Guilty Bystander*
—Thomas Merton

The trees stand watch over my day-to-day life. They are the guardians of my conscience. I have no one else to answer to, so I live and work under the generous but highly principled supervision of the trees—especially the deodars, who stand on guard, unbending, on the slope above the cottage. The oak and maples are a little more tolerant, they have had to put up with a great deal, their branches continually lopped for fuel and fodder. 'What would *they* think?' I ask myself on many an occasion. 'What would they like me to do?' And I do what *I* think they would approve of most!

Well, it's nice to have someone to turn to…

The leaves are a fresh pale green in the spring rain. I can look at the trees from my window—look down on them almost, because the window is on the first floor of the cottage, and the hillside runs away at a sharp angle into the ravine. The trees and I know each other quite intimately, and we have much to say to each other from time to time.

I do nearly all my writing at this window seat. The trees watch over me as I write. Whenever I look up, they remind me that they are there. They are my best critics. As long as I am aware of their presence, I can try to avoid the trivial and the banal.

Ramesh, the son of the municipal cleaner, looms darkly in the doorway. He is a stunted boy with a large head, but has wide gentle eyes. His orange-coloured trousers brighten up the surrounding gloom.

'What do you want, Ramesh?'

'Newspapers.'

'To sell to the kabari?'

'No. For wrapping my schoolbooks.'

'Well, take a few.' I give him half a dozen old newspapers, the headlines already look meaningless. 'Sit down and wait for it to stop raining.'

He sits awkwardly on a mora.

'And what is your cousin Vinod doing these days?' (Vinod is a good-looking ne'er-do-well who seldom does anything apart from hanging around cinema halls.)

'Nothing.'

'Doesn't he go to school?'

'He has stopped going to school. He got a job at fifty rupees a month, but he left after a week. He says he will join the army in September.'

The rain stops and Ramesh departs. The clouds begin to break up, the sun strikes the steep hill on my left. A woman is chopping up sticks. I hear the tinkle of cowbells. Water drips from a leaking drainpipe. And suddenly, clear and pure, the song of the whistling thrush emerges like a dark sweet secret from the depths of the ravine.

Bijju is back from school and is taking his parents' cattle out to graze. He sees me at the window and waves, then grabs his favourite cow Neelu by the tail and tells her to hurry up.

Bijju is twelve, a fair, good-looking Garhwali boy. His younger sister and brother are very pretty children. The father, an electrician, is a rather self-effacing man. The mother is a strong, hard woman. I have watched her on the hillside cutting grass. She has the muscular calves of a man, solid feet and heavy hands; but she is a handsome woman. They live in a rented outhouse further up the hill.

Bijju doesn't visit me very often. He is rather shy. But one day I looked out of the window and there he was in the branches of the oak tree, smiling at me rather hesitantly. We spoke to each other across the three or four yards that separate house from oak tree.

'If I jump, I can land in your tree,' I said.

'And if I jump I will be in your house,' said Bijju.

'Come on then, jump!'

But he shook his head. He was afraid of me. The tree was safe. He put his arms round the thickest branch and held himself close to it. He looked very right in the tree, as though he belonged there, a boy of the woods, a tree spirit peeping out from a house of glossy new leaves.

'Come on, jump!'

'*You* jump,' he said.

In the evening his sister brings the cows home. I meet her on the path above the house. She is only a year younger than Bijju, a very bonny girl who is going to be ravishingly beautiful when she grows up, if they don't marry her off too soon. She too has the same timid smile. But if these children are timid of humans, they are not afraid in the forest, and often wander far afield with Neelu the blue cow and others. (And S, who is eighteen and educated at an English-medium private school, wouldn't go alone into the forest if you paid him!) But the trees know their own. They will cherish the wild spirits and frighten the daylights out of the tame.

The whistling thrush is here, bathing in the rainwater puddle beneath the window. He loves this spot. So now, when there is no rain, I fill the puddle with water, just so that my favourite bird keeps coming.

His bath finished, he perches on a branch of the walnut tree. His glossy blue-black wings glitter in the sunshine. At any moment he will start singing.

Here he goes! He tries out the tune, whistling to himself, and then, confident of the notes, sends his thrilling full-throated voice far over the forest. The song dies down, trembling, lingering in the air; starts again, joyfully, and then suddenly stops, as though the singer had forgotten the words or the tune.

Vinod, the ne'er-do-well, turns up with a friend, asking me to give them some work. They want to go to the pictures but have no money.

'You can dig up this slope below the house,' I tell them. 'The soil is good for growing vegetables.'

This sounds too much like hard work for Vinod, who says, 'We'll come and do it tomorrow.'

'No, we'll do it now,' says his more enterprising friend, and to my surprise they set to work.

Now and then I look out of the window. They are digging away with fair enthusiasm.

After about half an hour, Vinod keeps sitting down for short rests, to the increasing irritation of his partner. They are soon snapping at each other. Vinod looks very funny when he sulks, because he has a snub nose, and somehow a snub nose and a ferocious expression only reminds me of Richmal Crompton's William. But the work gets done by evening and they are quite pleased with their earnings.

Bijju is right at the top of a big oak. The branches sway to his movements. He grins down at me and waves. The higher he is in the tree, the more confident he becomes. It is only when he is down on the ground that he becomes shy and speechless.

He has allowed the cows to wander, and presently his mother's deep voice can be heard calling, 'Neelu, Neelu!' (The other cows don't have names.) And then: 'Where is that wretched boy?'

Sir Edmund Gibson has come up. He spends the summer in the big house just down the road. He is wheezing a lot and says he has water in his lungs—and who wouldn't, at the age of eighty-six.

'Ruskin, my advice to you,' he says, 'is never to live beyond the age of eighty.'

'Well, once ought to be enough, sir.'

He is a big man, but not as red in the face as he used to be. His Gurkha manservant, Tirlok, has to push him up the steep slope to my gate.

Sir Edmund was once the British Resident in the Kathiawar states. He knew my parents in Jamnagar, when I was just five or six. He is a bachelor and is looked after by his servants.

His farm at Ramgarh doesn't make any money and he will probably give it to his retainers.

When Sir Edmund was Resident, he was once shot at from close range by a terrorist. The man took four shots and missed every time. He must have been a terrible shot, or perhaps the pistol was faulty, because Sir E presents a very large target.

He also treasures two letters from Mahatma Gandhi, which were written from prison.

'I liked Gandhi,' says Sir E. 'He had a sense of humour. No politician today has a sense of humour. They all take themselves far too seriously. But not Gandhi. He took his work seriously, but not himself. When I went to see him in prison, I asked him if he was comfortable, and he smiled and said, "Even if I was, I wouldn't admit it!"'

Sir E's servant brings tea, but there isn't any milk. I think I have exhausted Bijju's supply.

Now it's dusk and the trees are very still, very quiet. Far away I can hear the *chuk-chuk-chuk* of a nightjar. The lights on Landour hill come on, one by one. Prem is singing in the kitchen. There is a whirr of wings as the king crows fly into the trees to roost for the night. A rustling in the dry leaves below the window. A snake? Field rats? Porcupines? It is now too dark to find out. The day has ended, and the trees move closer together in the dark.

We are treated to one of those spectacular electric storms which are fairly frequent at this time of the year, late spring or early summer. The clouds grow very dark, then send bolts of lightning sizzling across the sky, lighting up the entire range of mountains. When the storm is directly overhead, there is hardly a pause in the frequency of the lightning; it is like a bright light being switched on and off with barely a second's interruption.

John Lang, writing in Dickens's magazine *Household Words* in 1853, almost exactly 120 years ago, had this to say about one of our storms:

> I have seen a storm on the heights of Jura—such a storm as Lord Byron describes. I have seen lightning, and heard thunder in Australia; I have, off Tierra del Fuego, the Cape of Good Hope, and the coast of Java, kept watch in thunderstorms which have drowned in their roaring the

human voice, and made everyone deaf and stupefied; but
these storms are not to be compared with a thunderstorm
at Mussoorie or Landour.

Forgotten today, Lang was a popular writer in the mid-nineteenth
century. He was also a successful barrister, who represented the
Rani of Jhansi in her litigation with the East India Company. He
spent his last years in Mussoorie and was buried in the Camel's
Back cemetery. His grave proved to be almost as elusive as his
books and I found it with some difficulty, overgrown with moss
and periwinkle. Prem and I cleaned it up until the inscription
stood out quite clearly.

Prem won't come home on a stormy night like this. He
is afraid of the dark, but more than that, he is afraid of
thunderstorms. It is as though the gods are ganging up against
him. So he will spend the night in the school quarters, where
he is visiting his mother who is staying there with relatives.

In the morning he turns up with a sheepish grin, saying it
got very late and he didn't want to wake me in the middle of
the night. I try to feign anger, but it is a gloriously fresh and
spirited morning; impossible to feel angry. A strong breeze is
driving the clouds away, and the sun keeps breaking through.
The birds are particularly active. The king crows (who weren't
here last year) seem to have taken up residence in the oaks. I
don't know why they are called crows. They are slim elegant
black birds, with long forked tails, and their call, far from being
a caw, is quite musical, though slightly metallic. The mynahs are
very busy, very noisy, looking for a nesting site in the roof. The
babblers are raking over fallen leaves, snapping up absent-minded
grasshoppers. Now and then, the whistling thrush bursts into
song, and then all other bird sounds pale into insignificance.
Bijju has taken his cows to pasture and now scrambles up the

hill, heading for home; he is late for school, and that is why he is in a hurry. He waves to me.

Both he and Prem have the high cheekbones and the deep-set eyes of the hill people. Prem, of course, is tall and dark. Bijju is small and fair; but he will grow into a sturdy young fellow.

The rain has driven the scorpions out of their rocks and crevices. I found one sitting on a loaf of bread. Up came his sting when we disturbed him. Prem tipped him out on the verandah steps and he scurried off into the bushes. I do not kill insects and other small creatures if I can help it, but there is a limit to my hospitality. I spared a centipede yesterday even though, last year, I was bitten by one which had occupied the seat of my pyjamas. Our hill scorpions and centipedes are not as dangerous as those found in the plains, and probably the same can be said for the people.

Prem tells me that his uncle is immune to scorpion stings, and allows himself to be stung in order to demonstrate his immunity. Apparently his mother was stung by a scorpion shortly before his birth!

Azure butterflies flit about the garden like flakes of sky.

Learnt two new words: bosky = wooded, bushy (bosky shadows); girding = jesting, jeering (girding schoolboys, girding monkeys).

Poor old Sir E is in a bad way. He has diarrhoea, and little or no control over the muscles that play a part in controlling the bowels. The Gurkha servant called me, and I went over with some tablets. Sir E looked quite exhausted and was panting from the exertion of walking from his bed to the toilet. The Gurkha is very good—gives Sir E his bath, dresses him, helps him on with his pyjamas.

Grateful for my alacrity in coming over with some medicine, Sir E offers me a whisky-and-soda (the first time he has ever done this), and pours himself a stiff brandy. He dozes off now and then, but the laboured breathing won't stop. He is a tough old tree, but I think he is beginning to find his massive frame something of a burden.

I make an attempt at conversation. 'Were you at Oxford or Cambridge?'

'Oxford. I joined Oxford in 1905 and left in 1909. Came out to India in 1910.'

He has an excellent memory, unlike Mr Biggs (a retired headmaster) who is ten years younger but will repeat the same story thrice in ten minutes.

'And when were you knighted?' I ask.

'1939 or 1940.'

He is too tired to do much talking. I let him doze off, and give my attention to the whisky. The log fire burns well, the flames cast their glow on Sir E's white hair and hanging jowls. The stertorous breathing grows in volume. He wakes up suddenly, complains that the fire is too hot; Tirlok opens the window. I finish the whisky; he doesn't offer another. It is his supper time, anyway, and I suggest soup and toast. 'Call me in the night if you have any trouble,' I say. He looks very grateful. The loneliness must press upon him a great deal.

I go out into the night. The trees are bending to a strong wind. From the foliage comes a deep sigh, the voice of leagues of trees sleeping and half disturbed in their sleep. The sky is clear, tremendous with stars.

For the first time this year I hear the barbet, a sure sign the summer is upon us. Its importunate cry carries far across the hills. It can keep this up for hours, like a beggar. Indeed, its plaint—*un-neow, un-neow!*—has been likened in the hills to that of the spirit of the village moneylender who has died before he can collect his dues. (*'Un-neow!'* is a cry for justice!)

It is difficult to spot the barbet. It is a fat green bird (no bigger than a mynah, but fatter), and it usually perches at the very top of a deodar or cypress.

The whistling thrush comes to bathe in the rainwater puddle. Sir E is much better and is sitting outside in the shade of an old oak. They are probably about the same age. What a rugged constitution this man must have; first, to survive, as a young man, all those diseases such as cholera, typhoid, dysentery, malaria, even the plague, which carried off so many Europeans in India (including my father); and now, an old man, to live and battle with congested lungs, a bad heart, weak eyes, bad teeth, recalcitrant bowels and god knows what else, and still be able to derive some pleasure from living. His old Hillman car is equally indestructible. But, like Sir E, it can't get up the hill any more; he uses it only in Dehradun.

I think his longevity is due simply to the fact that he refuses to go to bed when he is unwell. No amount of diarrhoea, or water in his lungs, will prevent him from getting up, dressing, writing letters or getting on with the latest Wodehouse (a contemporary of his) or *Blackwood's Magazine*, to which he has been subscribing for the last fifty years! He was pleased to find that some of my own essays were appearing in *Blackwood's*. Nothing will keep him from his four o'clock tea or his evening whisky-and-soda. He is determined, I am sure, to die in his chair, with all his clothes on. The thought of being taken unawares while still in his pyjamas must be something of a nightmare to him. (His favourite film, he once told me, was *They Died With Their Boots On.*)

The cicadas are tuning up for their first summer concert. Even Mrs Biggs, who is hard of hearing, can hear them. Yesterday I met her on the road above the cottage and exchanged pleasantries. Up at Wynberg the girls' choir was hard at practice.

'The girls are in good voice today,' I remarked.

'Oh yes, Mr Bond,' she said, presuming I meant the cicadas. 'They do it with their legs, don't they?'

◆

A week in Delhi. It is still only early summer, but the heat almost knocks one over. Slept on a roof, along with thousands of mosquitoes. It cools off in the early hours, but only briefly, before the sun comes shouting over the rooftops. The dust lies thick on floors, leaves, books, people. May's golden dust!

Now, back in the hills, I am struck first of all by the silence. The house, too, makes itself felt. It has been here too long not to have acquired a personality of its own. It is not a cheerful-looking place, nor is it exactly gloomy. My bedroom is rather dark (because it faces the abrupt slope of the hillside), but there is a wild cherry growing just outside the window—a cherry tree which I nurtured ever since it was a tiny seedling, five or six years ago, and which has now grown so tall that the branches tap against the roof whenever there is a breeze. It is a funny sort of cherry because it flowers in November instead of in the spring like other fruit trees. Small birds and small boys willingly eat the berries, which are too acid for adult palates.

The sitting room, with its two big windows looking out on the forest, is a bright room. Most of the wall space is taken up by my books. The rugs are worn and tattered—they have been with the house right from the beginning, I think—and I can't afford new ones.

On books and friends I spend my money;
For stones and bricks I haven't any.

Sir E, quite recovered from his recent illness, has gone down to Dehra again to attend to his farm and the demands of his farm workers. He should be back at the end of the month.

The brilliant blue-black of the whistling thrush shows up best when the sun is glinting off its back, but this seldom happens, because the bird likes to keep to the shade where it is almost black. Hopping about, it reminds me of Fred Astaire dancing in tophat and tails.

Now that it's getting hot, my small pool attracts a number of afternoon visitors—the mynahs, babblers, a bulbul, a magpie. After their dip they perch in the cherry tree to dry themselves and I can watch them without getting up from my bed, where I take an afternoon siesta. I reserve the afternoons for doing nothing. 'Silence and non-action are the root of all things,' says Tao. Especially on a drowsy afternoon.

But I haven't seen the whistling thrush for several days. Perhaps he is offended at having to share the pool which he was the first to discover. I haven't heard his song either, which probably means that he has moved down to the stream where it is cooler and shadier.

Prem's mother and younger sister come for a few days. His mother is a very quiet woman and doesn't say much even to her son. She is quite handsome, although she looks rather worn and tired, due probably to her recent illness.

His little sister, about four, is a friendly little gazelle; not in the least pretty, but lively and intelligent. She will have to stay here for at least six months to be properly treated for her incipient tuberculosis. There is no treatment to be had in their village.

While I am resting, still exhausted from an attack of hill dysentery (who called this a health resort?), Sir E blows in, red-faced, as distressed as a stranded whale. His Gurkha servant has walked out, after quarrelling with his wife and mother-in-law, and has taken with him his twin sons (aged one and a half). I calm Sir E, tell him Tirlok will be back in a day or two—he is probably trying to show how indispensable he is!

Sir E takes out a cigarette and strikes a match, and the entire matchbox flares up, burning a finger. Definitely not his day. I apply Burnol.

'It's all that damned girl's fault,' he says. 'She has a vile temper, just like her mother. We were very wise not to marry, Ruskin.'

Wise or not, I seem to have acquired a family all the same.

◆

Hundreds of white butterflies are flitting through the forest.

When Prem told his mother that I kept a human skull in my sitting room (given to me by Anil, a medical student, and *not* pinched from the cemetery as some suppose), she told him not to spend too much time near it. If he did, he would be possessed by the spirit of the woman who had originally inhabited the skull.

But Prem, at the present time, is immune to spirits, having succumbed to the charms of his young wife who stays downstairs with his mother. They have only been married a few months. He leans over the balcony, chatting with her; advises her on how to keep the courtyard clean; then makes her a small broom from the twigs of a wild honeysuckle bush. She enjoys all the attention she is getting.

The sky is overcast this morning. Dust from the plains has formed a thick haze which hides the valley and the mountains. We are badly in need of rain. Down in the plains, over 200 people have died of heatstroke.

I haven't seen Bijju for some days, but this morning his sister, Binya, was out with the cows. What a sturdy little girl she is; and pretty, too. I will write a story about her.*

---

*This story was called 'The Blue Umbrella'.

◆

'We'll take you to the pictures one day, Sir Edmund.'

'Yes, I must see one more picture before I die.'

So there comes a time when we start thinking in terms of the last picture, the last book, the last visit, the last party. But Sir E's remark is matter of fact. He is given to boredom but not to melancholy.

And he has a timeless quality. I have noticed this in other old people; they look more permanent than the young.

He sums it all up by saying, 'I don't mind being dead, but I shall miss being alive.'

A number of small birds are here to bathe and drink in the little pool beneath the cherry tree: hunting parties of tits—grey tits, red-headed tits and green-backed tits—and two delicate little willow warblers. They take turns in the pool. While the green-backs are taking a plunge, the red-heads wait patiently on the moss-covered rocks, coming down later to sip daintily at the edge of the pool; they don't like getting their feet wet! Finally, when they have all gone away, the whistling thrush arrives and indulges in an orgy of bathing, as he now has the entire pool to himself.

The babblers are adept at snapping up the little garden skinks that scuttle about in the leaves and grass. The skinks are quite brittle and are easily broken to pieces with a few hard raps of the beak. Then down they go! Babblers are also good at sifting through dead leaves and seizing upon various insects.

The honeybees push their way through the pursed lips of the antirrhinum and disappear completely. A few minutes later they stagger out again, bottoms first.

1 June

The dry spell continues. It is only before sunrise that there is any freshness in the air.

At dawn I said, 'Day, you will not begin without me.' I was up with the whistling thrush at five. The cicadas were tuning up, the crickets were already in full cry, and the whistling thrush was calling most sweetly. As none of these songsters could be seen, it was as though the forest itself was singing.

Feeling the dawn wind stir, I was happy that I had met the day at its very beginning.

When the sun came up, the day became sultry and oppressive. I had to walk two miles to Ban Suman and back. There was no shade anywhere along the road. But we are equipped with legs for the purpose of walking. As more and more people grow dependent on their cars, a new species of humans will evolve. Around the turn of the twenty-second century, I can see legless humans being born. By then, of course, there will be flying wheelchairs.

A pall of dust hangs over the mountain.

Someone asked Sir E if he could shoot a bird on his land at Ramgarh. The man wanted the bird for dissection in a biology lab. Sir E refused.

'It's in the interests of science,' protested the man. 'Do you think a bird is better than a human?'

'Infinitely,' said Sir E. 'Infinitely better.'

He goes down today to pay his farmhands. He will return in a few days unless it gets cooler in Dehra. He complains of being very bored up here, for he can't get about, and in Dehra he has his Hillman. 'I'm *rotting* with boredom,' he says.

Vinod, I hear, is laid low with a fever—the result of a day's hard work. He is now in retirement for the rest of the season.

Walked five miles down the Tehri road to Suakholi, where I rested in a small tea shop, a loose stone structure with a tin roof held down by stones. It serves the bus passengers, mule drivers, milkmen and others who use this road.

I find a couple of mules tethered to a pine tree. The mule drivers, handsome men in tattered clothes, sit on a bench in the shade of the tree, drinking tea from brass tumblers. The shopkeeper, a man of indeterminate age—the cold dry winds from the mountain passes having crinkled his face like a walnut—greets me enthusiastically, as he always does. He even produces a chair, which looks like a survivor from the Savoy's 1890 ballroom. Fortunately the Mussoorie antique dealers haven't seen it, or it would have been carried away long ago. In any case, the stuffing has come out of the seat. The shopkeeper apologizes for its condition: 'The rats were nesting in it.' And then, to reassure me: 'But they have gone now.'

Unlike the shopkeeper, the mule drivers have somewhere to go and something to deliver: sacks of potatoes. From Jaunpur to Jaunsar, the potato is probably the crop best suited to these stony, terraced fields. Oddly enough, it was introduced to the Himalayas by two Irishmen, Captain Young of Dehra and Mussoorie and Captain Kennedy of Simla, in the 1820s. The slopes of Young's house, Mullingar, were known as his Potato Farm. Looking up old books, I was surprised to learn that the potato wasn't known in India before the nineteenth century, and now it's an essential part of our diet in most parts of the country.

As the mule drivers lead their pack animals away, along the dusty road to Landour bazaar, I follow at a distance, singing 'Mule Train' in my best Nelson Eddy manner.*

A thunderstorm, followed by strong winds, brought down

*Not Nelson's song originally, but he sang it better than anyone else.

the temperature. That was yesterday. And today, June, it is cloudy, cool, drizzling a little, almost monsoon weather; but it is still too early for the real monsoon.

The birds are enjoying the cool weather. The green-backed tits cool their bottoms in the rainwater pool. A king crow flashes past, winging through the air like an arrow. On the wing, it snaps up a hovering dragonfly. The mynahs fetch crow feathers to line their nest in the eaves of the house. I am lying so still on the window seat that a tit alights on the sill within a few inches of my head. It snaps up a small dead moth before flying away.

Sir E is back. He found it too hot in the valley. Even up here he has given up wearing a necktie. I'll have him wearing a kurta and pyjamas before long; the only sensible dress in summer.

At dusk I sit at the window and watch the trees and listen to the wind as it makes light conversation in the leafy tops of the maples. A large bat flits in and out of the trees. The sky is just light enough to enable me to see the bat and the outlines of the taller trees. Up on Landour hill, the lights are just beginning to come on. It is deliciously cool, eight o'clock, a perfect summer's evening. Prem is singing to himself in the kitchen. His wife and sister are chattering beneath the walnut tree. Down the hill, a kakar is barking, alarmed perhaps by the presence of a leopard. All the birds have gone to sleep for the night. Even the cicadas are strangely silent. The wind grows stronger and the tall maples bow before it: the maple moves its slender branches slowly from side to side, the oak moves its branches up and down. It is darker now; more lights on Landour. The cry of the barking deer has grown fainter, more distant, and now I hear a cricket singing in the bushes. The stars are out, the wind grows chilly, it is time to close the window.

◆

Bijju is very much an outdoor boy, even when he isn't grazing cows. He isn't very strong in the chest, but his legs are sturdy; he was having no difficulty in scaling the high retaining wall. He grinned down at me. He is rather like the whistling thrush— absent for days, then unexpectedly reappearing in the forest or on the hillside. Bijju sings too, although his voice is more vigorous than melodic.

And that reminds me of the story of the whistling thrush. The bird was once a village boy who tried very hard to play the flute in the same style as the god Krishna. When the god heard his favourite melody being plagiarized, he was furious and turned the unfortunate boy into a bird. The whistling thrush still tries to copy the divine melody, but somehow it always breaks off right in the middle of a stanza. There ought to be a moral here, especially in a land full of plagiarists. Or to be fair, I should say film-land...

The Whistler. This is my name for the youth who labours part-time in the school. He is something of a character— scatterbrained, carefree, easy-going. He is always whistling— loudly and quite tunefully (this time a bird turned into a boy?)—so that you know when he's coming round a bend or through the trees, and even when it's dark you know who it is. He's usually out quite late, because he spends all his money at the pictures. He has three sisters, and they and the mother are all working as maids or ayahs, and as they are quite indulgent to him (the only brother) he doesn't have to work too hard. His shoes are always torn, even though his clothes look new.

He has a reputation for being a waster, but he returned the few rupees he borrowed from me last month. I suppose a youth who is always singing and whistling on the roads gives everyone the impression that he has nothing to do from morn till night, unlike that jolly miller of Dee who worked *and* sang the whole day through. (I know one man who forbids his children from singing in the home.)

But back to the Whistler, he is really quite enterprising. The other day he asked me for one of my books, and as I knew he hadn't squandered too many years in school, I gave him an easy Hindi translation of one of my children's books. But it was the paper he valued, not the words. He flogged it to the bania's small son, who took it apart and converted the large pages into envelopes, which were then used for selling gram and peanuts. In India it doesn't take long for anything to be recycled. On the way home, I saw a couple of customers throwing their empty packets away, and these were promptly consumed by a stray cow. There went my beautiful story!

Is there a lesson to be learnt from this? Yes. Don't give away complimentaries.

It rained all night, and the morning is cool and fresh. Parrots are on the wing. I feel like tap-dancing like Gene Kelly, but you can't tap dance on a hillside, you'd break an ankle. Only the roads (and not all of them) are suitable for a song-and-dance act, and no doubt the Whistler will oblige before long. At forty, I must refrain from being too frisky and boyish. But I'll do a reel in the garden when no one is looking.

24 June

The first day of monsoon mist. And it's strange how all the birds fall silent as the mist comes climbing up the hill. Perhaps that's what makes the mist so melancholy; not only does it conceal the hills, it blankets them in silence too. Only an hour ago the trees were ringing with birdsong. And now the forest is deathly still, as though it were midnight.

Through the mist Bijju is calling to his sister. I can hear

him running about on the hillside but I cannot see him.

Feeling sorry for Sir E (or maybe for myself), I walked over to see him. The door was closed, so I looked in at the French window (nothing could be more *English* than a French window, and no Agatha Christie mystery would be complete without one), I saw him sleeping in his chair with his chin on his chest. There was no dagger sticking out of his back, only a bit of stuffing from his old coat. My footsteps on the gravel woke him, and he got up and opened the door for me. He said he felt a bit tipsy; had taken his usual peg, but thought the quality of whisky varied from bottle to bottle, and wished he could lay his hands on a bottle of Scotch or even Irish. He could only offer me an Uttar Pradesh brand. I said I'd given up drinking, and this pleased him because in truth he hates anyone drinking his whisky; said he might give it up himself, it 'cost too damn much'! I told him it would be unwise to give up drinking at this stage of his life. As he had reached the age of eighty-six on two pegs a day, he was obviously thriving on it. Giving it up now would only play havoc with the orderly working of his system. I'd given it up in order to help an alcoholic friend abstain, and also because I wanted to give up *something*, and strong drink seemed the easiest thing to do without.

A cicada starts up in the tree nearest my window seat. What has he been doing all these weeks, and why does he choose this particular moment and this particular evening to play the fiddle so loudly? The cicadas are late this year, the monsoon has been late. But soon the forest will be ringing with the sound of the cicadas—an orchestra constantly tuning up but never quite getting into tune—and the sound of the birds will be pushed into the background.

Outside the front door I found an elegant young praying mantis reclining on a leaf of the honeysuckle creeper. I say young because he hadn't grown to his full size, and was that very tender pale green which is the colour of a young mantis. They are light brown to begin with, like dry twigs, but as they grow older and the monsoon foliage becomes greener, they too change, and by mid-August they are dark green.

◆

As though to make up for lost time, the monsoon rains are now here with a vengeance. It has been pouring all day, and already the roof is leaking. But nothing dampens Prem's spirits. He is still singing love songs in the kitchen.

Kailash, whom I have known for a couple of weeks, asks me for twenty-five rupees.

'What do you need it for?' I ask.

'It's for my Sanskrit teacher,' he says. 'I have failed in Sanskrit but if I give the teacher twenty-five rupees he'll alter my marks. You see, I've passed in all the other subjects, but if I fail in Sanskrit I'll fail the entire exam and remain a pre-Inter student for another year.'

I took a little time to digest this information and ponder on the pitfalls of the examination system.

'He must be failing a lot of boys,' I said. 'Twenty-five rupees each! Are there many others?'

'Some. But he dare not fail the good ones. They can ask for a recheck. It's the borderline cases like me who give him a chance to make money.'

This placed me in a quandary. Should I yield to the evils of the examination system and provide the money for pass-marks? Or should I adopt a high moral stance and allow the boy to fail?

Whatever the evils of the exam system, they are not the fault of the student. And either way he isn't going to turn into a great Sanskrit scholar. So why be a hypocrite? I gave him the money.

Kailash slogs in his uncle's orchard all morning, gets a midday meal (no breakfast), and hasn't any shoes. And yet his uncle, a member of one of Garhwal's well-known upper-caste families, is a wealthy man.

Kailash tells me he will return to his village once he knows his result. According to him his uncle is such a miser that at mealtimes he pauses before each mouthful, wondering: 'Ought I to eat it? Or should I keep it for tomorrow?'

I am visited by another kind of student, a small girl from one of the private schools. Her mother has brought her to me for my autograph.

'She studies your book in Class six,' I was informed.

'And what book is that?' I asked the little girl.

'Tom Sawyer,' she replied promptly. So I signed for Mark Twain. When a small storeroom collapsed during the last heavy rains, I was forced to rescue a couple of old packing cases that had been left there for three or four years—since my arrival here, in fact. The contents were well soaked and most of it had to be thrown away—old manuscripts that had been obliterated, negatives that had got stuck together, gramophone records that had taken on strange shapes (dear 'Ink Spots', how will I ever listen to you again?*)... Unlike most writers, I have no compunction about throwing away work that hasn't quite come off, and I am sure there are a few critics who would prefer that I throw away the lot! Sentimental rubbish, no doubt. Well, we can't please everyone; and we can't preserve everything either. Time and the elements will take their toll.

But a couple of old diaries, kept in exercise books almost twenty years ago, had managed to survive the rain, and I put them out in the sun to dry, and then, almost unwillingly, started

---

*This was before the advent of audiotapes.

browsing through them. It was instructive, and sometimes a little disconcerting, to discover the sort of person I had been in my twenties. In some ways, no different from what I am today. In other ways, radically different. A diary is a useful tool for self-examination, particularly if both diary and diarist are still around after some years.

One particular entry caught my eye, and I reproduce it here without any alteration, because it represented my credo as a young writer, and it set me wondering if I had lived up to my own expectations. (Nobody else had any expectations of me!)

The entry was made on 19 January 1958, when I was living on my own in Dehradun:

> The things I do best are those things I do on my own, alone, of my own accord, without the advice or approval of others. Once I start doing what other people tell me to do, both my character and creativity take a dip. It is when I strike out on my own that I succeed best.
>
> There was a time when I was much younger and poorer than I am now. I had been over a year in Jersey, in the Channel Islands; I was unhappy, and the atmosphere in which I was writing was one of discouragement and disapproval. And that was why I wrote so well—because I was defiant! That was why I finished the only book I have finished so far. I had to prove to myself that I could do it.
>
> One night I was walking alone along the beach. There was a strong wind blowing, dashing the salt spray in my face, and the sea was crashing against the St Helier rocks. I told myself: I will go to London; I will take up a job; I will finish my book; I will find a publisher; I will save money and I will return to India, because I can be happier there than here.

And that was just what I did.

I had guts then.

What's more, I had an end in view.

The writing itself is not enough for me. Success and money are not enough. I had a little of both recently,* but they did not help me to do anything wonderful. I must have something to write for, just as I must have something to live for. And that's something I have yet to find.

There was more in that vein, but I give this excerpt as an example of a young man's determination to be a writer in what were then adverse circumstances. Thirty-five years later, I'm still trying.

27 June

The rains have heralded the arrival of some seasonal visitors—a leopard; and several thousand leeches.

Yesterday afternoon the leopard lifted a dog from near the servants' quarters below the school. In the evening it attacked one of Bijju's cows but fled at the approach of Bijju's mother, who came screaming imprecations.

As for the leeches, I shall soon get used to a little bloodletting every day. Bijju's mother sat down in the shrubbery to relieve herself, and later discovered two fat black leeches feeding on her fair round bottom. I told her she could use one of the spare bathrooms downstairs. But she prefers the wide open spaces.

Other new arrivals are the scarlet minivets (the females are yellow), flitting silently among the leaves like brilliant jewels. No matter how leafy the trees, these brightly coloured birds cannot

---

*When *The Room on the Roof* was published (1956).

conceal themselves, although, by remaining absolutely silent, they sometimes contrive to go unnoticed. Along come a pair of drongos, unnecessarily aggressive, chasing the minivets away.

A tree creeper moves rapidly up the trunk of the oak tree, snapping up insects all the way. Now that the rains are here, there is no dearth of food for the insectivorous birds.

In spite of there being water in several places, the whistling thrush still comes to my pool. He, at least, is a permanent resident.

Kailash has a round, cheerful face, only slightly marred by a swivel eye. His hair comes down over his forehead, hiding a deep scar. He is short, but quite compact and energetic. He chatters a good deal but in a general sort of way, and a response isn't obligatory.

It's quite possible that he will go away as soon as he gets his exam results. He's fed up with being the Cinderella of his uncle's house. He tells of how his miserly uncle went to see a rather permissive film, and was very shocked and wanted to walk out, but couldn't bear the thought of losing his ticket money; so he sat through the film with his eyes closed.

Sir E departed for Dehra with his large retinue of servants and their dependants, all of whom would have done justice to an eighteenth-century nabob. 'I am at the mercy of my servants,' he told me the other day.

But he had placed himself at their mercy long ago, by setting himself up as a country squire surrounded by 'faithful retainers'—all of whom received generous salaries but did little or no work. If he sold his white elephant of a farm, he'd be quite comfortable with one servant.

'I'll probably come up in September, after the rains,' he said. 'If I live that long... I'm just living from day to day.'

'So am I,' I told him. 'It's the best way to live.'

A couple of days passed before Kailash came to see me. I

was beginning to wonder if he'd come again. Apparently the teacher had at first proved elusive; but the deed was done, and Kailash passed with the marks he needed. Ironically, his uncle was so impressed that he is now urging the boy to remain with him and complete the Intermediate exam.

'I must write a story about your uncle,' I remark.

'Don't give him a story', says Kailash. 'A short note will do.'

Now that Prem is preoccupied with his wife, and the house is at the mercy of uninvited visitors, I stay out most of the time, and these days Kailash is my only companion. Yesterday we took Camel's Back Road, past the cemetery. He chatters away, and I can listen if I want to, or think of other things if I don't want to listen; apparently it makes no difference to him. He is a cheerful soul, with an infectious laugh. He walks with a slight swagger, or roll. He says he doesn't mind staying here now that he has me for a friend; that he can put up with two sour uncles as long as he knows I'm around. I suspect he's quite capable of pulling a fast one on his uncle; but all the same, I find myself liking him.

Moody. And when I'm moody I'm bad.

Prem says: 'It is easier to please God than it is to please you.'

'But God is easily pleased,' I respond. 'God makes absolutely no demands on us. We just imagine them.'

The eyes.

Prem's eyes have great gentleness in them.

His wife's eyes are round and mischievous and suggestive...

Suggestive enough to invite the attention of a mischievous or malignant spirit.

At about two in the morning I am awakened by Prem's shouts, muffled by rain. Shouting back that I am on my way, for it is obviously an emergency, I leap out of bed, grab an umbrella, dash outside and then down the stairs to his room.

His wife is sobbing in bed. Whatever had possessed her has now gone away, and the crying is due more to Prem's ministrations—he exorcizes the ghost by thumping her on the head—than to the 'possession' itself. But there is no doubt that she is subject to hallucinatory or subconscious actions. It is not simply a hysterical fit. She walks in her sleep, moves restlessly from door to window, holds conversations with an invisible presence, and resists all efforts to bring her back to reality. When she comes out of the trance, she is quite normal.

This sort of thing is apparently quite common in the hills, where people believe it to be a ghost taking temporary possession of a human mind. It's happened to Prem's wife before, and it also happens to her brother, so it seems to run in families. It never happens to Prem, who deeply resents the interruption to his sleep.

I calm the girl and then make them bring their bedding upstairs. I give her a sleeping tablet and she is soon fast asleep.

During a lull in the rain, I hear a most hideous sound coming from the forest—a maniacal shrieking, followed by a mournful hooting. But Prem and his wife sleep through it all. The rain starts again, and the shrieking stops. Perhaps it's a hyena. Perhaps something else.

A morning of bright sunshine, and the whistling thrush welcomes it with a burst of song. Where do the birds shelter when it rains? How does that frail butterfly survive the battering of strong winds and heavy raindrops? How do the snakes manage in their flooded holes?

◆

I saw a bright green snake sunning itself on some rocks; no doubt waiting for its hole to dry out.

In my vagrant days, ten to fifteen years ago (long before the hippies made vagrancy a commonplace), I was a great frequenter of tea shops, those dingy little shacks with a table and three chairs, a grimy tea kettle, and a cracked gramophone. Tea shops haven't changed much, and once again I find myself lingering in them, sometimes in company with Kailash, who, although he doesn't eat much, drinks a lot of tea.

One can sit all day in a tea shop and watch the world go by. Amazing the number of people who actually do this! And not all of them unemployed. The tea shop near the clock tower is ideal for this purpose. It is a busy part of the bazaar but the tea shop, though small, is gloomy within, and one can loll about unseen, observing everyone who passes by a few feet away in the sunlit (or rain-spattered) street. The tea itself is indifferent, the buns are stale, the boiled eggs have been peppered too liberally. Kailash is unusually quiet; there is no one else in the shop. People who would stop me in the road pass by without glancing into the murky interior. This is the ideal place; not as noble as my window opening into the trees, but familiar, reminiscent of days gone by in Dehra, when cares sat lightly upon me simply because I did not care at all. And now perhaps I have begun to care too much.

I gave Bijju a cake. He licked all the icing off it, only then did he eat the rest.

◆

It was a dark windy corner in Landour bazaar, but I always found the old man there, hunched up over the charcoal fire on which he roasted his peanuts. He'd been there for as long as I could remember, and he could be seen at almost any hour of the day or night. Summer or winter, he stayed close to his fire.

He was probably quite tall, but we never saw him standing up. One judged his height from his long, loose limbs. He was very thin, and the high cheekbones added to the tautness of his tightly stretched skin.

His peanuts were always fresh, crisp and hot. They were popular with the small boys who had a few paise to spend on their way to and from school, and with the patrons of the cinemas, many of whom made straight for the windy corner during intervals or when the show was over. On cold winter evenings, or misty monsoon days, there was always a demand for the old man's peanuts.

No one knew his name. No one had ever thought of asking him for it. One just took him for granted. He was as fixed a landmark as the clock tower or the old cherry tree that grew crookedly from the hillside. The tree was always being lopped; the clock often stopped. The peanut vendor seemed less perishable than the tree, more dependable than the clock.

He had no family, but in a way all the world was his family, because he was in continuous contact with people. And yet he was a remote sort of being; always polite, even to children, but never familiar. There is a distinction to be made between aloneness and loneliness. The peanut vendor was seldom alone; but he must have been lonely.

Summer nights he rolled himself up in a thin blanket and slept on the ground, beside the dying embers of his fire. During the winter, he waited until the last show was over, before retiring to the rickshaw-coolies' shed where there was some protection from the biting wind.

Did he enjoy being alive? I wonder now. He was not a joyful person; but then, neither was he miserable. I should think he was a genuine stoic, one of those who do not attach overmuch importance to themselves, who are emotionally uninvolved, content with their limitations, their dark corners. I wanted to get to know the old man better, to sound him out on the immense questions involved in roasting peanuts all his life; but it's too late now. The last time I visited the bazaar the dark corner was deserted; the old man had vanished; the coolies had carried him down to the cremation ground.

'He died in his sleep,' said the tea-shop owner. 'He was very old.'

Very old. Sufficient reason to die.

But that corner is very empty, very dark, and whenever I pass it I am haunted by visions of the old peanut vendor, troubled by the questions I failed to ask; and I wonder if he was really as indifferent to life as he appeared to be.

◆

Prem brought his wife some of her favourite mangoes. This afternoon he took her into my room so that she could listen to the radio. They both fell asleep at opposite ends of the bed; are still asleep as I write this in the next room, at my window. If I curled up a little, I could fall asleep here on the window seat. Nothing would induce me to disturb those innocents; they look far too blissful in their slumbers.

◆

Kailash and I are caught in a storm and it's by far the worst storm of the year. To make matters worse, there is absolutely no shelter for a mile along the main road from the town. It was fierce, lashing rain, quite cold, whipping along on the wind from all angles. The road was soon a torrent of muddy water, as earth and stones came rushing down the hillsides. Our one umbrella was useless and was very nearly blown away. The cardboard carton in which we were carrying vegetables was soon reduced to pulp. We broke into a run, although we could hardly see our way. There were blinding flashes of lightning—is an umbrella a good or a bad conductor of electricity? Kailash sees humour in these situations and was in peals of laughter all the way home, even when we slid into a ditch.

He takes my hand and holds it between his hands. He is happy. He has got his self-confidence back, and can now deal with his uncles and Sanskrit teachers.

In the morning I work on a story. There is a dove cooing in the garden. Now it is very quiet, the only sound is the distant tapping of a woodpecker. The trees are muffled in ferns and creepers. It is mid-monsoon.

Kailash, his hair falling in an untidy mop across his forehead, drags me out of the house and over the wet green grass on the hillside. I protest that I do not like leeches, so we make for the high rocks. He laughs, talks, chuckles, and when he grins his large front teeth make him look like a 1940s' Mickey Rooney. When he looks sullen (this happens when he talks about his uncle), he looks Brando-ish. He has the gift of being able to convey his effervescence to me. Am I, at thirty-eight, too old to be gambolling about on the hill slopes like a young colt? (Am I, sobering thought, going to be a character of enforced youthfulness like the man on the boat in *Death in Venice?* Well, better that than the Gissing hero of *New Grub Street* who's old at forty.) If I am fit enough to gambol, then I must gambol. If I can still climb a tree, then I must climb trees, instead of just watching them from my window. I was in such high spirits yesterday that I kept playing the clown, and I haven't done this in years. To walk in the rain was fun, and to get wet was fun, and to fall down was fun, and to get hurt was fun.

'Will it last?' asks Kailash.

'This feeling of love between us?'

'*This* won't last. Not in this way. But if something *like* it lasts, we should be happy.'

◆

Prem is happy, laughing, giggling all the time. Sometimes it is a little annoying for me, because he is obviously unaware of what is happening around him—such as the fact that part of the roof blew away in the storm—but I am a good Taoist, I say nothing, I wait for the right moment! Besides, it's a crime to interfere with anyone's happiness.

Prem notices the roof is missing and scolds his wife for seeing too many pictures. 'She's seen ten pictures in two months. More than she'd seen in her whole life, before coming here.' She pulls a face. Says Prem: 'My grandfather will be here any day to take her home.'

'Then she can see pictures with your grandfather,' I venture. 'While we repair the roof.'

'I wouldn't go anywhere with that old man,' she says.

'Don't speak like that of my grandfather. Do you want a beating? Look at Binya'—we all look at Binya, who is perched very prettily on the wall—'she hasn't seen more than two pictures in her life!'

'I'll take her to the pictures,' I offer.

Binya gives me a radiant smile. She'd love to go to the pictures, but her mother won't allow it.

Prem relents and takes his wife to the pictures.

Binya's mother has a bad attack of hiccups. Serves her right, for stealing my walnuts and not letting me take Binya to the pictures.

In the evening I find Prem teaching his wife the alphabet, using the kitchen door as a blackboard. It is covered with chalk marks. Love is teaching your wife to read and write!

◆

These entries were made in 1973, twenty years ago.

The following year I did not keep a journal, but these are

some of the things that happened:

Sir E had a stroke and, like a stranded whale, finally heaved his last breath. According to his wishes, he was cremated on his farm near Dehra.

To Prem and Chandra was born a son, Rakesh, who immediately stole my heart—and gave me many a sleepless night, for as a baby he cried lustily.

Kailash went into the army and disappeared from my life, as well as from his uncle's.

Bijju and Binya were to remain a part of the hillside for several years.

DEHRA DUN—WINTER OF '45

It snowed in Dehra that winter—on the evening of the 2nd of January, the day after another baby half-brother was born.

Normally it did not snow in Dehra. You had to look up to the Mussoorie range, to see the white-crested peaks after the first snowfall. For it to snow in the valley was quite freakish.

It came down quite suddenly, while I was returning from one of my walks. Soon the lichi and guava trees were covered with a soft mantle of snow. Dehra had never looked prettier—I ran indoors to tell my mother. She was in bed with the baby.

'It's snowing outside, Mum!' I cried excitedly.

'I don't feel like joking just now, Ruskin,' she said. 'I'm very tired.'

So I ran outside, plucked a snow-covered twig off one of the lichi trees and took it inside to show my mother. She looked pleased and brightened up considerably.

Next morning there was lots of snow lying around, and I played snowballs with my stepfather's mechanic and some of the neighbourhood boys. Then the sun came out, and by noon the snow had vanished.

The following day I went to see Miss Kellner. She told me that it had snowed in Dehra forty years earlier, when she had first arrived in the town. Now perhaps it was a sign that she should go away.

'Don't go,' I said. 'Wait for the next snowfall.'

So we played 'Snap' and I finished all her ginger biscuits.

Then she was carried indoors for her bath. As she couldn't stand up, or even straighten up, she had to be bathed by her ayah. But she never missed her daily bath; it had become a sort of ritual with her.

She had her own personal rickshaw and four liveried men to pull it. As she couldn't climb into tongas or cars, she had to use the rickshaw. She was only a featherweight and the rickshawmen flew down the road with her; I couldn't keep up with them. She enjoyed these rides and took one every evening. The rickshaw was painted sky blue.

Her parents had left her a fair amount of money; otherwise she could not have afforded these luxuries. And she could not have survived without them. But her mind was far from being crippled. She possessed all her faculties—which was more than could be said for many who had the use of all their limbs.

During the War years Dehra was a lively little town. It had been made a recreational centre for war-weary Allied troops, and there were large contingents of British and American solders stationed on the outskirts. As a result, cafés, dance-halls, bars and even a couple of 'nightclubs' sprang up all over the place, and the subsequent revelry continued until the early hours of each morning.

My mother and Mr Hari went out almost every night. The old Ford convertible would bring them back at two or three in the morning. My insecurity was such that I would often wonder how I would cope if they had a fatal accident coming home, or if some avenging tigress got her own back in the jungle. Would I have to look after my sister, baby brother and two half-brothers? And where would the money come from?

Money did not seem to be a concern with my mother and stepfather. There seemed to be plenty of it around and I presumed Mr Hari's motor workshop was flourishing.

But my instincts were sound and my fears not without foundation; for I returned from one of my afternoon walks to find all our boxes, bedding, furniture, pots and pans, out on the driveway. Apparently there were several months' arrears of rent due to the landlord, and he had secured an eviction order.

We ended up in Granny's house—poor soul, she was much put out, her cherished privacy shattered by her youngest daughter's unconventional lifestyle—and stayed there for the remainder of my winter holidays.

◆

Spring came to the foothills in February, and Dehra's gardens were at their best then. Masses of sweet peas filled the air with their delicious scent; bright yellow California poppies formed a carpet of their own; scarlet poinsettias greeted each other over hedges and garden walls; snapdragons of many hues gave off their own elusive scent; bright red poppies danced in the slightest breeze. Those were the days when houses and bungalows had spacious compounds, with space for flower and vegetable gardens and even orchards. Over the years the pressures of population and the demand for more living space has meant the disappearance of large gardens. Some of the old bungalows survive in the middle of cramped housing estates, and there is little room left for flowers and fruit trees except up at Rajpur or parts of Dalanwala. Miss Kellner told me that Granny's sweet peas used to win prizes at the annual flower show (held every year in the first week of March), but after Grandfather's death (when I was just two), she seldom exhibited her flowers. Dhuki, who had been with her many years, continued to look after the garden.

Miss Kellner did not take much interest in the garden but her little sitting room was crowded with bric-a-brac: ornate vases, decorative wall-plates, china figurines, little wooden toys... It was impossible to move around without knocking something over, so her visitors wisely stuck to her dining room or verandah or, better still, sat out beside her under the pomalo tree, while she shuffled her cards or did her hisaab (the day's accounts) or scribbled notes to her friends.

All this was a far cry from the feverish nightlife of the 'Casino' or the 'White House' or 'Green's,' where roistering soldiers on leave gathered late in the evenings to dance with the few Anglo-Indian girls who still lived in Dehra and were looking for a little fun and maybe even romance. These dances often ended in drunken brawls, sometimes between British and American servicemen. The latter were better paid and free with their money, and this led to some resentment.

One of these girls, a pretty little thing called Doreen, had fussed over me whenever my mother had taken me to the store below the Casino, where she worked. She must have been eighteen or nineteen. I couldn't help noticing that she had lovely legs and full sensuous lips that I longed to kiss. :

One evening she invited me to accompany her to a dance up at the Casino, and my mother and stepfather making no objection, I escorted her into the restaurant-cum-ballroom where the local band was playing the latest Glenn Miller hits. The hall was full of tobacco smoke and beer fumes. Doreen gave me a glass of rum, which I downed without any hesitation. I then led her on to the dance floor, much to everyone's delight. An eleven-year- old doing the foxtrot with one of the town beauties must have been a sight to behold. Unfortunately, the next dance went to one of the "'Tommies' (soldiers), and soon she was bestowing her favours on the entire contingent of Allied troops in the dance hall while I moodily played with a plate of fish fingers that had been placed in front of me.

However, came the midnight hour—it was New Year's Eve—
and the lights went off, and while everyone sang 'Auld Lang
Syne,' Doreen gathered me in her perfumed arms and planted
a long sweet kiss on my hungry lips.

It was my first real kiss and I savour it still.

◆

I heard later that Doreen married one of her soldier boys and
went to live in one of London's working-class districts.

The exodus of British and Anglo-Indian families was
beginning even as the War ended. For some the choice was a
hard one. They had no prospects in England, no relatives there.
And they had no prospects in India unless they were very well
qualified. For many Anglo-Indians and 'poor whites,' assisted
passages to England were the order of the day. By the time
1947, the year of Indian Independence, came around, most of
these people had gone, to make some sort of living in the U.K.
The rush to Australia took place much later.

I suppose I qualified as a 'poor white.' But there were many
whose circumstances were much worse than mine.

Take Mrs Deeds and her seventeen-year-old son, Howard.

I met them in the winter of '45-'46, at which time my
mother was managing the Green's Hotel (it has long since
vanished) just off Rajpur Road. My stepfather's showroom
and garage had closed down (for the second time) and he was
once again living with his first wife, who now ran her own
grocery store. My mother had taken a manager's job, running
the Green's Hotel, which had seen better days. Her modest
salary helped to keep us all going, although, fortunately, my
school fees were being paid by the RAF, which also sent an
allowance for my sister.

The Green's was a well-laid out bungalow-type hotel with

about twenty rooms, but in those days it was rare for more than two or three of them to be occupied. The post-War slump had already hit Dehra. This lean period was to continue into the early fifties.

My mother had allowed me to occupy one of the small single rooms at the back of the hotel for the duration of my holidays. Occupying the next room was Mrs Deeds, in her late thirties, and her teenager son, with all their possessions. God knows where they had come from, or why they had come to Dehra. They had no friends or relatives in the town. They were the flotsam of Empire, jettisoned by the very people who had brought them into existence. There were many such down-and-outs.

A good-looking woman was Mrs Deeds, but an alcoholic. When she was hitting the bottle, her son ridiculed her, and they had the most terrible fights. He was a self-righteous youth who blamed his mother for the situation they were in—without support (for she had been deserted by her husband), without a home (for that had been sold for a song), and without any prospects (for there was no one to turn to). Her feeling of guilt was compounded by her son's attacks on her, and as a result she hit the bottle with renewed vigour.

When she was broke, she would cadge a drink from my mother. When he was broke, he would borrow the odd rupee from me.

She could not pay her bills at Green's and had to leave. They took up residence in the second-class waiting room at the railway station. An indulgent stationmaster allowed them to stay there for several weeks; then they moved into a cheap, seedy little hotel outside the station.

Mrs Deeds, like Mr Micawber, was always expecting a 'remittance' from the man who'd bought her property in Naini Tal but had yet to pay the main amount. She'd sold her wedding ring and gold watch to pay for drink and the rent. Howard loafed around, talking big. When they got to England or Australia or wherever they were going, he'd find a job to his liking. It did not occur to him to look for one in Dehra.

Late one evening, after Mrs Deeds had been drinking at a small liquor shop near the clock tower, she set out to cross the maidan to see someone at the club who had promised her some help. She was set upon by a gang of three or four young men who beat her badly and then raped her. Although she cried out for help, no one came to her assistance. The maidan had always been a safe place; but times were changing.

My mother went to see her and gave her what help she could. Then the remittance (or part of it) arrived, and Mrs Deeds and her son went their way and presumably started a new life abroad.

◆

I went to see Miss Kellner.

There she was, hunched up in her garden chair, making the most of her restricted life—broken nose, twisted hands, shattered feet—scribbling little notes to her friends and then inviting me to a game of 'Snap'.

No one was going to rape Miss Kellner.

Or, for that matter, Mrs Kennedy, another piece of human flotsam, now in her sixties and engaged by my mother to look after Ellen.

Mrs Kennedy was a widow, Irish as her name suggests. Unlike Mrs Deeds, she had fond memories of her husband, who had died when quite a young man. He was a beautiful singer, according to Mrs Kennedy; sang everything from opera to Irish ballads. She gave me her own rendering of Danny Boy' in a warbling contralto but lost the melody half-way through and ended on a cracked note.

'Did you sing duets?' I asked.

'No, he preferred singing alone.'

I wasn't surprised but refrained from saying so.

'He was a tenor—sang like John McCormack,' she told me.

Personally, I preferred a robust baritone like Nelson Eddy or Laurence Tibbett, but to please her I went through an album of old records and found one of McCormack singing 'When Irish Eyes are Smiling.' We discovered a small wind-up gramophone in one of the hotel rooms, and she took it to her room and played the record over and over again.

She was tall and angular and I don't think she could ever have been good-looking, but I enjoyed listening to her. Older people have always found me a patient and sympathetic listener. Sometimes they are inclined to ramble on, but if you listen carefully, you will often find that they have some interesting tales to tell.

But my sister Ellen took a strong dislike to Mrs Kennedy, as indeed she did to anyone who was put in charge of her. A backward child with defects of vision and the first signs of epilepsy, she had very strong likes and dislikes. For instance, she hated bananas, and if Mrs Kennedy tried to reason with her by saying, 'Bananas are good for you, dear, bananas would fly about the room and everyone present would have to duck for cover.

Anything that was 'Good for her' was immediately resented and cast aside. Ellen longed to be a bad girl, but she was to retain for all her life the mind of a six-year-old.

'Brain cutlets, I informed her one day as this delicacy arrived on the dining table. 'Bad for you. You're not supposed to eat them.'

She immediately devoured three brain cutlets and asked for more. To this day she loves brain cutlets, under the impression that they will make her very wicked.

Mrs Kennedy, however, decided to leave us the day she received a grapefruit in her eye. Ellen did not see straight, and on this occasion she was really aiming at me (I had been teasing her); but the grapefruit, thrown with considerable force, struck Mrs Kennedy instead.

She went to work as a dormitory matron in a local convent school, and as a parting present I gave her the John McCormack record.